This Web site is

Josh hit a few buttons, and a list of Web sites came scrolling across the screen. That was when I saw it: ccc.timesolvers.com.

I nudged Josh. "Go on, click on it. I want to see if that weird guy from the TV commercial appears."

"Okay." Josh clicked the mouse.

A swirling maze of numbers filled the screen. In the center were the words *Do you need more time?* I couldn't tear my gaze away. I felt as if I were being hypnotized.

Do you need more time? The question flashed on the screen again. Beneath it appeared two boxes labeled *Yes* and *No*.

I clicked on the *Yes* box.

A cartoon figure of Professor Chronos appeared. He looked exactly like the guy from the TV commercial. A cartoon bubble floated over his head.

Hello, Chris Fenton. How can I help you today?

I blinked in amazement. How did a cartoon character inside a computer know my name?

CYBER ZONE

Double Trouble

CYBER ZONE

Double Trouble

S. F. Black

Art direction by Fabia Wargin.
Cover art by Broeck Steadman.

Printed in the United States of America.

10 9 8 7 6 5 4 3 2 1

Chapter 1

"All right, Chris," my band teacher, Mr. Delgado, barked. His brown eyes bored into mine like two laser beams. "What's your excuse for being late this time?"

I gulped. I had an excuse, a good excuse, but I'd been late for band practice three times in a row. I could tell by the look in Mr. Delgado's eyes that he'd just run out of patience.

"Sorry, Mr. Delgado," I stammered. "I had basketball practice. Coach O'Rourke scheduled an extra practice this afternoon because we've got a big game coming up against Wolverhampton." I didn't mention that Coach O'Rourke had chewed me out in front of the whole team for leaving basketball practice early to go to band practice.

"Chris, I've heard that line from you too many times before," Mr. Delgado snapped. "Maybe it's time you decided which is more important to you—basketball or music. You can't be in two places at once, you know."

"Yes, Mr. Delgado," I mumbled. "It won't happen again. I promise."

I slid into my seat. Glaring at me, he continued, "You have to learn to honor your commitments!"

"Yes, Mr. Delgado," I said again. I pulled my trumpet case onto my lap.

"All right, let's get started," Mr. Delgado growled. "Time is precious, and we can't afford to waste it!"

The room grew silent as everyone waited for me to get ready. I sneaked a peek at my music teacher. I couldn't believe the way he was acting. Mr. Delgado usually smiles a lot and makes jokes. In fact, he sometimes wastes half the practice making jokes. That's one reason he's my favorite teacher. But today Mr. Delgado seemed to be all business.

I swallowed guiltily. The reason he was in such a bad mood had to be me. It was true. I was never on time—at least, not lately. And practice couldn't start without me because I was the star trumpet player. I had two big solos in the spring concert, which was coming up in just a few days.

"Chris, what are you waiting for?" Mr. Delgado demanded. "Didn't you hear me? We can't afford to waste any more time."

"Yes, sir!" Quickly, I flipped up the locks on my trumpet case and began to assemble my trumpet.

"Way to go, Chris," my best friend, Josh, whispered behind me. Josh plays the French horn. "I can't believe you managed to make Mr. Delgado mad!"

I glanced back at him and grimaced. Josh didn't grimace back. He just gave me a stern look. Suddenly it seemed as if the whole world was mad at me—my music teacher, my coach, even my best friend. Probably Josh was still mad at me because I'd been late for his birthday party last week—so late that I'd missed the pizza *and* the cake. I'd apologized a million times, and Josh had almost forgiven me—I thought.

If only I could be in two places at once, I glumly reflected, remembering a commercial I'd seen on TV the night before. In the ad a weird-looking guy named Professor Chronos was standing in front of a big clock. "Do you ever feel like there aren't enough hours in the day?" he had asked in this really serious, intense voice. "Do you ever wish you could be in two places at once?" Then he'd smiled. "Now you *can*. Just call TimeSolvers at 1-900-666-TIME or visit our Web site: *ccc.timesolvers. com*. Soon your scheduling problems will be solved forever."

I'd begged my mom to let me call, but she'd just shaken her head. "No way, Chris. That commercial is just a scam. Besides, do you have any idea how much it costs to dial a nine-hundred number?"

"But Mom," I'd answered. "I definitely have serious scheduling problems. I'll pay for it from my allowance!"

"Oh, Chris," my mom had said. "You do not have scheduling problems. You just need to get better organized, that's all."

Easy for her to say, I thought gloomily as I set my sheet music out on the stand. She wasn't trying to juggle band practice, basketball, and tons of homework.

Deep down I knew Mom was right—of course it would help if I were better organized. Like Josh. Josh was organized, and so was his younger sister, Jenna. They always looked good, their rooms were always clean, and they always knew where to find everything.

Not me. My mom says that *disorganized* should be my middle name. My room is a disaster. I never know where anything is, and I'm not the neatest dresser in the world, either. Mr. Delgado once told me not to worry about it, that creative people were often messy. The way he'd said it had made me feel proud. I might be messy, but I was creative.

Suddenly, though, I had the feeling that even Mr. Delgado wished I would clean up my act. Out of the corner of my eye, I saw him raise his bushy eyebrows as I searched frantically for my trumpet mouthpiece. Why hadn't I put it in my case, like I was supposed to? I rummaged through my backpack and finally found the mouthpiece at the bottom, along with a bunch of old pens and pencils. The mouthpiece had some ink on it. I wiped it off with my T-shirt.

"Well, now that Chris finally has his trumpet together, maybe we can get started," Mr. Delgado said sarcastically.

I bit my lip. I couldn't believe my favorite teacher was so mad at me. That's when I decided that whatever it took, things were going to be different. No longer would I be messy, late, disorganized Chris Fenton. Instead, I would be tidy, on time, and on top of everything—even if it meant that I really did need to be in two places at once.

As Mr. Delgado raised his baton for us to start, I smiled to myself. Everyone who knew me was going to get a big surprise when they met the new, improved Chris Fenton. But the way things turned out, the one who got the big surprise—okay, the shock of his life—was me.

Chapter 2

"**B**oy, was Mr. Delgado ticked off at you," Josh said as we left the band room after practice. "I've never seen him that mad before. It was like he was a different person."

I groaned. "Don't remind me."

But Josh was on a roll. "Did you notice he didn't crack one single joke the whole practice? That's not like him, even when he's mad."

"Maybe he had a personality transplant," I muttered, "or maybe he just ran out of patience."

"But he acted so mean." Josh's voice was doubtful. "He's never yelled at Karen Ellis like that." Karen Ellis was a sixth grader who played third clarinet in the band. She had to be about the worst musician who ever lived.

Josh was right. Usually Mr. Delgado was really patient, even when Karen made horrible mistakes. But today he'd been on her case about little things. At one point she'd burst into tears and run out of the band room.

"Maybe he thinks I should do better because—well, I'm more serious about music," I said.

"Your problem is that you're serious about too many things," Josh said. "Except people's birthday parties."

I studied his expression. He'd tried to pass it off as a joke, but I could tell he was still really hurt. I couldn't blame him. Turning thirteen is a big deal.

"Josh, look," I said. "I'm really, really sorry about your party, okay? I promise I'll never let you down like that again."

"I've heard you say that before, Chris."

"But this time I really and truly mean it."

"Yeah, yeah." He flapped his hands to imitate a mouth blabbing away.

"Josh, listen. I'm turning over a new leaf, I swear," I went on, trying to convince him. "From now on, I'm going to get organized. This afternoon I'm going to clean up my room, and—"

A grin creased Josh's face. "That I'd like to see," he said.

"I'm serious!" I protested.

"You mean you're going to get rid of all those six-month-old sandwiches under your bed?"

"I do *not* have old sandwiches under my bed!" I declared. "Well, okay, but they're probably only four months old," I said a second later.

"At least five," Josh insisted.

I ignored him. "Anyway, I'm going to clean up the whole thing this afternoon," I went on. I didn't mention that my mom had said I *had* to clean my room in the next day or two. "And then I'm going to . . ." My heart sank as I remembered something.

It had happened again. I'd been so busy with basketball practice, my trumpet solos, and making amends to Josh that I had forgotten about my history presentation. Tomorrow in class I was supposed to talk about the Pilgrims. Personally, I think the Pilgrims are really boring. But my history teacher, Ms. March, is crazy about them. She says that they're a fascinating example of people attempting to create a utopian society.

"You're going to what?" Josh prompted.

"Never mind," I told him. "I just remembered—I have my stupid history presentation tomorrow."

Josh grinned. "I guess that means you'll have to hit the library this afternoon."

"Nope." I shook my head. "The computer Dad ordered for me finally arrived, and last night he hooked up the modem. I'm officially on-line." Normally, I would have told Josh about my new computer right away, but it had come the weekend after I'd missed his birthday party. Josh hadn't been talking to me then.

"You're joking!"

"No, I'm not. Dad finally finished setting everything up for me."

Josh's green eyes began to glow like a cat's. "Cool," he said. "Now we can trade e-mail and play games and stuff!" He slapped me on the back. "Congratulations, Chris. Welcome to the twenty-first century!"

As crazy as I am about basketball and music, Josh is even crazier about computers. When he grows up he wants to be a computer programmer, or maybe a computer designer. Since we're best friends, you'd think I'd be into computers, too, but the truth is, I don't know the first thing about them. In fact, when my dad told me he'd bought me a computer, I'd been disappointed at first. I'd been hoping for a new trumpet.

Josh and I stopped at my locker before heading home. As I dialed my combination, Josh was still talking about my new computer. "As soon as I get home, I'll send you some e-mail," Josh declared.

"I don't think I've got an e-mail address yet," I mumbled.

"What?" Josh shook his head and laughed. "You're hopeless, Chris. I'll bet you haven't even turned the computer on yet."

"Well . . ."

"You want me to come over and show you how to use it?"

I grinned. "I was hoping you'd offer, but I didn't want to ask."

"I'm always ready to show off my stellar computer skills," Josh bragged. Next we went over to his locker, where he stuffed some books into his backpack. Then his face fell. "Oh, I forgot. I promised Jenna I'd help her with her algebra this afternoon."

"She can come, too," I suggested.

"Come where?" a voice suddenly demanded. We turned around. Josh's sister stood behind us.

"Chris's house," Josh explained. "He has a new computer. I'm going to help him set it up while I help you with your homework."

"That's cool," Jenna said. "Sure, I'll come along."

Jenna flashed me a smile, and I felt my face turn hot. I would never let Josh know this in a million years, but I think Jenna is really cute. She's a year younger than us, and she's small and skinny, with brown hair and eyes so blue that they almost don't look real. She doesn't look anything like Josh, and her personality is different, too. While Josh is into computers and math, Jenna wants to be a writer when she grows up. She's always taking notes in this big old notebook she carries around with her.

Josh closed his locker. We were about to head for the door when something occurred to me—Jenna was going to see the total disaster area otherwise known as my room.

"What's wrong, Chris?" Jenna asked. She must have noticed the panicked look on my face.

"Maybe I should clean my room before you guys see it," I blurted out.

"What for?" Jenna said cheerfully. "I already know what a slob you are. Dirty laundry everywhere. Six-month-old sandwiches under the bed."

I turned on Josh. "You told her about that?" I said indignantly.

"Well, I—"

"What kind of friend are you?"

"It's okay. Josh once had some year-old cookies stashed in his mattress," Jenna informed me.

"What kind of sister are you?" Josh said, pretending to punch her in the shoulder.

Jenna just laughed. Josh and Jenna get along really well. Not like me and my younger brother, Eddie. His favorite name for me is *dorkface*. Eddie is seven, and his hobby is thinking of new ways to drive me crazy.

When Josh, Jenna, and I got to my house, Mom wasn't home from work yet. But Eddie was there, and so was our babysitter, Mrs. Walker. "Hi, kids. Want some milk and cookies?" Mrs. Walker called from the kitchen.

Eddie smirked at me. "Hey, Chris, I thought Mom said you weren't supposed to have any friends over until you cleaned up your room."

I reached out my hand, pretending to swat him.

"Now, Chris." Mrs. Walker raised her eyebrows at me. "Is what Eddie says true?"

I squirmed. "*Um . . .*"

"It's okay, we're here to help Chris clean his room," Jenna piped up. I gave her a grateful look.

"Wow, you must be nuts. I wouldn't touch that mess," Eddie chimed in.

I ignored his obnoxious comment, grabbed a plate of cookies, and headed upstairs with my friends. I led them into my room. In the afternoon sunlight it looked like a disaster even to me. I hoisted a pile of shirts off the top of the computer and turned it on. Josh sat down eagerly in front of the screen.

He spent a few minutes pressing buttons and reading instructions that appeared on the screen. Jenna stood behind him, reading over his shoulder. Finally, I heard the modem activate with a screechy hiss, followed by several beeps.

"There," Josh announced proudly as he stood up. "Now you've got an e-mail address." Then I sat down, and he showed me how to send and receive e-mail. I was surprised the whole thing was so easy.

"Okay," Josh said. "Let's pull up some Web sites."

He hit a few more buttons, and a list of Web sites came scrolling across the screen. "What's your topic for the history presentation again?" he asked.

"Pilgrims," I replied unenthusiastically. That was when I saw it: *ccc.timesolvers.com.*

Jenna pointed to the address. "I saw a commercial for that," she said. "It looks like the site for you, Chris."

"I already asked my mom if she'd let me call the number, but she wouldn't," I admitted. I nudged Josh. "Go on, click on it. I want to see if that weird guy from the TV commercial appears—Professor Chronos, or whatever his name is."

"Okay." Josh reached over and clicked the mouse.

A swirling maze of numbers filled the screen. In the center were the words *Do you need more time?* For some reason, I suddenly felt nervous. I told myself to relax, then skooched my chair closer. I couldn't tear my gaze away while the numbers swirled around and around in front of my eyes. I felt as if I were being hypnotized.

Do you need more time? The question flashed on the screen again. Beneath it appeared two boxes labeled *Yes* and *No*.

"Go on, Chris. Click *Yes*," Jenna said impatiently.

So I clicked on the *Yes* box. Sure enough, a cartoon figure of Professor Chronos appeared.

"There he is!" I declared. He looked exactly like the guy from the TV commercial. But as I watched him, something really weird happened. Professor Chronos gave me an odd, eerie smile, and a cartoon bubble appeared over his head.

Hello, Chris Fenton, I'm Professor Chronos. How can I help you today?

I blinked in amazement. How did a cartoon character inside a computer know my name?

Chapter 3

The Professor Chronos cartoon character was still smiling strangely at me. Another bubble appeared over his head. *Chris, do you need more time?* it said. *Welcome to the TimeSolvers Web site! If time management is a problem for you, just take our simple TimeSolvers quiz. In a few minutes, you'll be on your way to solving your scheduling problems forever!*

I stared at the screen with my mouth open.

"Chris, what's wrong?" Jenna said from beside me.

"How does this Professor Chronos guy know my name?" I demanded.

Jenna shrugged. "The Web site must have gotten your name from your e-mail address."

"But Josh just put that address on the Net a few minutes ago," I countered.

"He's right," Josh said, frowning. "Besides, the e-mail address I chose isn't his whole name. It's *ChrisFen*, not *Fenton*."

"Well, there has to be some kind of logical explanation," Jenna said. She turned to me. "Have you ever logged onto this Web site before?"

"Are you kidding?" I asked. "I've never even logged onto the Internet before."

Josh's frown deepened. "That's strange. Maybe

someone's playing a joke on you, Chris."

"Like who?" I asked. "How would anyone know that I might log onto this Web site?"

Then I blinked. Another bubble had appeared over the cartoon figure of Professor Chronos. *So, Chris, are you ready to take our TimeSolvers quiz?*

"Don't take it," Jenna said quickly. "Just click *Exit* and get out of there."

"Why? What's wrong with taking a simple quiz?" Josh asked.

"This is creepy," Jenna murmured. "I think we should just exit and explore another Web site. Let's find a Pilgrim one so you can do your report, Chris."

I had the creeps, too. Still I couldn't resist clicking *Start Quiz*.

"I'm going to check it out," I said. "I can always exit if I want."

Jenna just shrugged.

My computer went blank and then made a funny buzzing noise. I thought I'd pushed the wrong button and messed up my Internet connection until a page of writing flashed onto the screen.

The TimeSolvers quiz was just a bunch of simple questions, like the surveys in one of those dumb ladies' magazines that my mom sometimes buys. Quickly, I read the first question.

You have an important social engagement, but you also have a big project due at school. You:

a. Try to reschedule the social engagement. After all, your friends can wait.
b. Turn the paper in late. When you get right down to it, school just isn't as important as friends.

c. Try to do both. Sure, you'll have to stay up late, but you're used to burning the midnight oil.

Whoever wrote this must be ancient, I thought. My grandfather said stuff like "burning the midnight oil." Still, *c* was definitely the right answer for me, so I clicked on it. With Josh and Jenna reading over my shoulder, I raced through the rest of the questions. They were pretty easy to answer, stuff like: *How often during a single week do you wish you could be in two places at once? Never, Sometimes,* or *Always.* I picked *Always,* of course. A few minutes later the quiz was complete.

As I entered my last answer, the computer started making that funny whirring sound again.

"What do you bet it just tells you what you already know?" Josh said.

"What's that?" I asked.

"That it's time for you to decide what your priorities are," Josh replied, imitating Mr. Delgado.

I laughed. But Jenna gasped, drawing her breath in sharply. "I don't believe this!" she exclaimed as she stared at my computer.

Josh and I looked at the screen. Professor Chronos was back, with a new bubble over his head. This one read: *Your answers to our quiz have convinced us that the only way to solve your scheduling problems is to employ the services of a double. As a one-time special introductory offer, we are willing to offer you one copy of yourself, free of charge. Your double will be accurate in every detail, as well as efficient and energetic. Complete satisfaction guaranteed. Do you wish to take advantage of this offer?*

I rubbed my eyes to make sure I wasn't dreaming, but, sure enough, the offer was still there, with two boxes underneath. One said *Yes*, and the other one said *Cancel*.

"*Hmm*," Josh murmured, rereading the screen. "This is pretty bizarre."

I glanced over at him. His forehead was all wrinkled up, and he was rubbing his hands together eagerly, like a mad scientist.

Suddenly a lightbulb went on in my brain. Josh was the one playing the joke! It had to be him. He was a whiz at computers. He'd probably made up this whole program just to freak me out—and get revenge on me for missing his birthday party.

But how had Josh found out I'd gotten my new computer? Then it clicked. Eddie must have told him. My little brother couldn't stand me, but he worshipped Josh. He'd probably blabbed about my computer when Josh wasn't speaking to me.

"Ha-ha, Burnett," I blurted out as I clicked on the *Yes* button. "I bet you think you're pretty clever. But did you have to go this far to convince me I've got major problems managing my time?"

Before Josh could reply, the computer started making a weird noise again. This time the noise was even louder and stranger than before. It was so loud it made the whole machine shake.

My computer sounded as if it were about to blow up!

A beam of blindingly bright light suddenly leaped out of the screen. To my horror, it was focused right on me! The light scanned my whole body, and I felt like I was being X-rayed from the top of my head to the tips of my toes. I closed my eyes and tried to move out of the light's path, but I couldn't. I was paralyzed.

"Help," I gurgled. "Josh, come on. Make it stop!"

Instantly, the light faded.

"Pretty funny," I said, glaring at Josh. "That light hurt . . ." My voice abruptly trailed off. Josh looked as white as a sheet, and his green eyes were as round as the eyes of an owl.

"Chris, you've got to believe me!" he said in a choked voice. "I had nothing to do with this!"

Chapter 4

Suddenly, Jenna let out a squeal. "Look!" she hissed.

Josh and I swiveled to face the monitor. A message was blinking in the middle of the screen.

"Copy successfully completed," I read aloud. I was still trying to figure out what it meant when the message vanished. Professor Chronos's face appeared again. He was grinning, a crooked, knowing smile that sent chills up my spine. Then a new cartoon bubble appeared over his head. *Good-bye, Chris, and good luck!* The screen went blank, and a moment later the start-up prompt appeared in the top left corner.

"That's funny," Josh said. "We've been bumped off-line."

"Never mind that. What did it mean by 'Copy successfully completed'?" asked Jenna.

That's exactly what I was wondering. I was horrified as I turned to my friends. "Maybe it meant what it said. Maybe the TimeSolvers program somehow copied me," I croaked.

"Chris, give me a break. It has to be a scam of some kind," Josh said.

"But why would anyone pull a scam like that?" I demanded.

Josh shrugged. "Who knows? There are all kinds of wackos on the Internet."

"Put us back on-line," Jenna said urgently. "I want to go to that Web site again. Maybe we can find out more about Professor Chronos."

"Like why he has that weird name," I said.

Jenna turned to me, her blue eyes solemn. "It's actually the perfect name for him. *Chronos* was the name of the ancient Greek god of time."

I stared at her for a minute. "Time? You mean as in TimeSolvers?"

"Bingo," Jenna said. She pushed me aside and started punching away at the keyboard. She wasn't a computer nut like Josh, but she knew her way around the Internet, which was more than I could say for myself. I wished yet again that my dad had bought me a new trumpet instead of a computer.

"How do I list Web sites again?" Jenna asked her brother.

"Hit *List*," Josh replied.

"Let's just forget it, Jenna," I said. I was feeling a little panicky, but I was trying my best not to show it, especially in front of her.

What if the message were true? What if I had been successfully copied? What if there really were two of me? Thinking about it made my head spin.

Beside me, Jenna leaned closer to the computer. "It's not there!" she cried.

"What's not there?" I asked.

"The listing for TimeSolvers." Jenna jabbed a finger at the screen. "Check it out for yourself. The Web site is gone!"

I looked at the names scrolling across the screen.

Jenna was right. There were listings for *Time* magazine, *Time Slaves* (whatever that was), and *Time Temporaries.* But no *TimeSolvers*.

The whole Web site had vanished!

Chapter 5

Another chill went up my spine, but I was still acting like it was no big deal. "I guess that proves Josh was right," I said with a shrug. "TimeSolvers must be some kind of scam. Maybe Professor Chronos—or whoever this person is—just likes freaking people out on-line or something."

"You're probably right," Josh said, sounding relieved. "Do you still want to do your Pilgrim research?"

"Maybe later," I quickly replied. "I think I've had enough Net surfing for now." I switched off the machine. For a moment, the three of us eyed one another nervously.

"So what should we do?" Jenna ventured.

"Help Chris get a start on cleaning this room," Josh said, a wicked gleam in his eye. I felt better now that he was teasing me again. "He said he was turning over a new leaf."

I looked around at the piles of junk covering every surface. "Yeah, I did say that," I admitted. "But I lied. Let's go to the kitchen and get more cookies instead," I suggested. "I'm starving!"

"Me, too," said Jenna. "Mrs. Walker's oatmeal raisin cookies are totally awesome."

We all trooped downstairs and loaded up on cookies. Then we went into the den to watch TV. Eddie was watching some boring nature program for little kids called *Our Friends in the Animal Kingdom*. But because Josh was there, he didn't complain when we wanted to change the channel.

We turned on the Super Sci-Fi Film Festival that was running on Channel 36. One of my favorite movies was on: *Alien Invasion from Planet B*. It's this really cool flick about aliens who look like giant slugs. They take over the world and turn all the people into robotlike slaves.

I'd seen the movie at least five times, and I'd always enjoyed it. This time I didn't, though. The plot kept making me think about the TimeSolvers site and Professor Chronos. I knew I was probably letting my imagination run wild, but what if I really had been copied? It was impossible, but what if I had? Would I turn into some robot or alien or something?

I tried to imagine what it would be like if there were two of me. In a way it would be awesome. I wouldn't have to stand up in Ms. March's class and make an idiot of myself talking about Pilgrims. I could make my double do it. He could clean my room and do my homework, too. On the other hand, the whole idea was so fantastic that it made me feel dizzy—and even sort of scared.

By the time the movie ended, it was pretty late. Jenna stood up and said she had to get home and tackle her math homework.

As I walked my friends to the front door, I started getting really worried that I *had* been copied. Josh didn't seem to notice how I was feeling, but Jenna did. "Hey, Chris," she said softly. "Let us know if anything, you know, *happens,* okay?"

"Don't sweat it. Nothing is going to happen," I answered.

I must have sounded pretty convincing, because Jenna's face relaxed into a smile. "You're probably right. See you tomorrow."

"See you," I echoed.

When they were gone, I wandered restlessly around the house. It was as if I were waiting for something to happen, but nothing did. Mom and Dad came home from work, and Mom told Eddie and me to set the table. In the short time it took to lay out the plates and silverware, my brother called me *moron, dorkface,* and *bat breath* about fifty times. In a way it felt good to be fighting with him, as if everything were normal. And by the time dinner was over, I'd almost forgotten about Professor Chronos and his offer to send me a free double.

I helped clean up the kitchen and then trudged upstairs to do my Pilgrim research. At first I was worried that it would be hard to find anything about the Pilgrims on the Internet, but it wasn't. You wouldn't believe how many Pilgrim nuts there are out there: people who are all excited about the fact that their great-great-grandparents came over here on the *Mayflower* or whatever.

An hour later I had more than enough stuff for my presentation. I snickered to myself as I considered calling my report "Why the Pilgrims Were Such a Pain."

Ms. March would sure love that title, I thought as I exited the Web site. I was about to switch off my computer when a message flashed across the screen: *E-mail waiting.*

I felt a surge of excitement. "E-mail. Cool!" Josh or

Jenna must have sent me a note. Eagerly I clicked on the icon to retrieve my very first piece of e-mail.

As the words filled the screen, I wondered why my friends had written such a long message. But when I started to read it, I realized it was just one word repeated over and over.

Beware, beware, beware, beware . . .

Chapter 6

There was no signature or address from the sender, so I had no way of knowing who the message was from. *Was it Josh?* I wondered. Maybe he really had tried to play a joke on me with the TimeSolvers Web site. But then I remembered Josh's face when the bright light came bursting out of my computer. Josh had looked as stunned as I felt. *No way he could have acted that well,* I told myself. *Right?*

I stared at the e-mail message. *Beware.* Beware of what? Professor Chronos? Mr. Delgado kicking me out of the band? Coach O'Rourke kicking me off the team? I scowled. One thing was certain—I already had plenty to worry about without getting any mystery warnings.

It has to be Josh, I decided. He was getting back at me for missing his party. I guess I couldn't really blame him.

Then I remembered something. When I'd seen the commercial for TimeSolvers on TV, Professor Chronos had given out the nine-hundred number *and* the Web site address. I let out a long breath. That meant there was no way Josh could be playing a joke on me. The TimeSolvers Web site was real.

I stared at the blinking computer screen as panic gripped me. I tried desperately to calm down. Just because the TimeSolvers Web site was real didn't mean it could really copy a person. No one could do that!

I switched off my computer and took a deep breath. It hadn't exactly been the greatest day of my life. More like the worst, I decided as I staggered down the hall to the bathroom to brush my teeth. But tomorrow was definitely going to be better. I knew no one believed me, but I was going to get myself organized. Tomorrow, I'd do a great job in history class, be on time for basketball practice, and practice my trumpet solos for the spring concert. Maybe I'd even finally get my room cleaned.

With that thought I went back to my room and climbed into bed. Before shutting off my light, I set my alarm for six o'clock.

The next thing I knew, sunlight was streaming into my eyes. I blinked and turned to look at my alarm clock. "Oh, no!" I gasped, sitting up in a hurry. It was after eight o'clock! Why hadn't the alarm gone off?

So much for my new start. I'd overslept by two hours!

The strange thing was, I didn't feel as if I'd slept that long. Maybe that was because all night long I'd had weird dreams. In one of them, Professor Chronos had been chasing me around the basketball court, yelling "Time, time, time!" But he was still a cartoon figure, just like he'd been on the computer, and no one else had noticed him.

"Oh, man," I groaned. I couldn't believe how late it was. Why hadn't Mom or Dad come in to wake me up? Usually they were banging on my door if I overslept by five minutes.

I leaped out of bed and searched around frantically for some clean clothes. Yes! Mom had left some clean laundry outside my door. I yanked on a pair of jeans and a red-striped T-shirt. Then I pulled on some white socks. I'd worn them once, but they weren't too grungy. I stuck my feet in my basketball shoes, grabbed my backpack, headed for the door, ran back to my desk to get my notes for my history presentation, and bounded out of the room.

Whew! The day had barely started and I was already out of breath. I trotted to the top of the stairs.

The house seemed unusually quiet.

"Mom?" I called softly. I was about to ask her why she hadn't woken me up like she usually did. Then I heard Mom talking to someone in the kitchen.

"Thanks for walking Eddie to school this morning, Chris," she was saying. "Are you sure you don't mind? I don't want you to be late."

Chris? She was talking to me? I grabbed the banister to steady myself.

"No problem, Mom. I have plenty of time today," a kid's voice replied. The voice sounded geeky but also eerily familiar.

"I'm really grateful, Chris."

"I told you, Mom, no problem."

The hair on the back of my neck stood up. The voice sounded familiar because it *was* familiar. It was *my* voice!

"See you tonight," I heard myself say.

All at once, I had that funny feeling you get when someone tapes your voice, or you hear yourself on someone's answering machine, and all you can think about is how dorky you sound. But this feeling was much weirder than that.

Slowly, I started down the steps. I froze halfway down the staircase.

A boy walked out with Eddie trailing behind him. Eddie had a grumpy expression on his face—as usual—

but the older boy was smiling broadly. He was wearing jeans with a hole in the left knee and a T-shirt that looked a lot like the one I had on—except it had red and blue stripes. His hair was brown, his eyes were greenish-brown, and freckles were splashed across his nose. He was tall and skinny—he was *me*! Right down to the cowlick on the top of his head.

I wanted to call out to him, but my voice felt as if it had dried up in my throat. Inside my brain, three words played over and over: *Copy successfully completed*. Now I knew the truth. I *had* been copied. I had a real-life double!

Just then, the boy glanced up the stairs. I drew back, but I could tell he'd spotted me. As our eyes met, he didn't say anything. He just winked at me, very slowly and deliberately.

A wink can be friendly, but this one seemed threatening. It was as if he was telling me—no, warning me—to keep quiet.

Then he turned away. "Come on, Eddie," he said loudly. "We'll be late for school. Let's go."

Eddie looked nearly as startled as I was. "What's up with you today, dorkface?" he demanded suspiciously. "Why are you being so nice?"

My double's grin made my blood run cold. "Because you're my brother, Eddie," he replied.

This guy really is *a dorkface,* I thought as the back door closed behind them.

In the kitchen, I could hear my mom whistling to herself. She sounded happy. *Almost as if she likes him— whoever he is—better than she likes me,* I thought with a flash of jealousy. Then I shook my head. It was crazy to feel jealous. It was crazy to feel anything. In fact, the whole thing was just plain crazy. I took a cautious step forward. *Maybe I'm dreaming,* I thought.

But just then, I ran my hand down the banister. A splinter the size of a giant elm tree lodged itself in my palm. *Yowee!* Did it ever hurt!

I smothered a yelp. Nothing that had happened to me in my dreams had ever hurt this much. That could only mean one thing: I wasn't dreaming. I had a double.

A double who at this very minute was walking my little brother to school. Or was he? What if he was an alien like the ones in *Alien Invasion from Planet B?* What if he was planning to kidnap Eddie and turn him into a robotlike slave?

I clutched my backpack. There was only one thing to do. I had to follow them—fast! I tiptoed down the stairs, through the kitchen, and down the hallway to the front door. I turned the knob. But just as I was about to pull it open, I heard a sound behind me.

"Chris!" my mom cried. "I thought you'd left. What are you doing back here? Where's Eddie?"

Chapter 7

"*Uh* . . ." I licked my lips as my mother stood in the front hallway looking at me, hands on her hips. "Eddie's outside," I lied. "I just came back because . . . er . . . I forgot the notes for my history presentation."

"Oh," Mom said, and then she sighed. "I might have known you'd forget something, Chris. Well, you'd better get going, or you and Eddie will be late."

"Sure, Mom! See you." I slipped out the door. I felt relieved, but also hurt. *I might have known you'd forget something!* Why did my mom always have to say stuff like that?

"Because it's true," I muttered aloud. I glanced up the street. Far ahead, I could see Eddie walking along beside my double.

They seemed to be heading for the school. *Maybe this copy isn't an alien invader after all,* I thought with relief. *Maybe he really is taking Eddie to school.*

Suddenly I smiled. Seeing a mirror image of myself had flipped me out so much, I had forgotten about all the good things I'd imagined yesterday. From now on, *my double* could walk my bratty little brother to school instead of me. We could totally split my busy schedule. With a little coordination, it would work out great. He'd be in charge of dealing with Eddie, doing my math homework, and researching my boring history presentations. I could concentrate on the things I liked—practicing trumpet and playing basketball. My teachers would be happy. My mom and dad would be happy. Everyone would be happy.

I'd be the new, improved Chris Fenton, just like I'd promised myself I would be. All I had to do was have a talk with my double—figure things out so we wouldn't ever both be in the same place at the same time.

I sped up. "Hey, wait!" I called out. Then I clapped my hand over my mouth. I had to talk to my double, but not in front of my little brother. I could just imagine what a fuss Eddie would make if he found out there were two of me. He'd probably tell my parents, and I'd have to send my double back.

I hesitated, wondering what to do. Then I decided I'd better just follow my double and Eddie to school. As soon as I got the chance, I'd catch my double's attention and find someplace where we could talk alone.

I crept along the hedges of the houses, watching Eddie and my double as they walked down the street half a block or so ahead of me. I felt like a spy—only I was spying on myself. My double walked fast, swinging his arms back and forth.

That must be how I walk, I thought. I'd never seen myself walk before. My double turned his head and said something to Eddie, who started laughing. I couldn't believe it. I could never make Eddie laugh. He never even laughed when I told him my best jokes.

I knew it was silly, but I felt a little jealous for the second time that morning. My double was just like me. He walked like me. He talked like me. Still, there was something different about him. I looked down at myself and realized what it was. Compared with me, my double was neat and organized-looking. He had his shirt tucked in, while mine was pulled out. His shoelaces were tightly tied, while one of mine had come undone. His hair was combed, while mine—I knew without looking—was sticking up all over my head. No wonder Mom seemed to like him better.

My double was a new, improved me. He was everything I'd dreamed about becoming. But somehow, instead of making me feel good, this made me feel pretty bad.

Up ahead, my double and Eddie turned the corner. I streaked after them. When I reached the corner, they had already crossed the street and were strolling through the gates of Jackson Elementary and Middle School.

The first bell was about to ring. I could tell because kids were arriving from all directions. I watched my double mingle easily among them.

I wondered what I should do now. If I ran up to the school, everyone would see there were two of me. How could I explain that?

On the other hand, what was I supposed to do? Cut school?

As I stood hidden in the lilac bushes, trying to make up my mind, the bell rang. In seconds, the playground was deserted. Cautiously, I ran across the street. Maybe my double had dropped Eddie off and was now waiting for me on the playground. I figured he must want to talk to me as badly as I wanted to talk to him. After all, he'd been created to help me. He probably needed to know what to do next.

I hurried into the playground and looked around, but

my double wasn't anywhere to be seen. The second bell rang. I headed for the school steps. I'd have to track my double down later. Right now, I needed to get to homeroom or I'd be late again. And if I was late again, I'd get detention for sure.

I tore up the steps and raced down the hall. I stopped at my locker, opened the lock in five seconds flat, and threw my backpack inside. Still clutching the notes for my history presentation, I ran to the door of my homeroom. I stopped outside the closed door. Someone was reading the announcements. "Lunch today will be corn dogs and okra succotash." I made a face. Our school cafeteria makes the worst lunches in the whole world. I started to open the door. Then I caught a glimpse of a familiar face in the front row.

It was me. Or, rather, my double.

He was sitting right in front of Ms. Nelson's desk, his notebook neatly open in front of him. I never sat right in front of Ms. Nelson. I always sat in the back.

What a goody-goody, I thought in disgust, squinting at him through the door's glass window. I took a step backward. If he was sitting in my homeroom, where was I supposed to go? How did he know where my homeroom was, anyway?

Then I figured it out. Since he was my double, he knew everything I knew. I slunk down the hall, my mind in a whirl. Having a double to help me organize my life was one thing, but being replaced by a double was another. And that was how I felt: replaced. How could I have ever imagined that two of me would be better than one?

"Chris Fenton!" a voice snarled behind me.

I turned around, and then I wished I hadn't.

It was our assistant principal, Mr. Broadus. In most schools the principal is mean, but our principal, Ms. Baker, is really nice and easygoing. It's our assistant principal who's the monster. Mr. Broadus is always giving kids detention—even for stupid stuff like talking during assembly or eating in the halls. Right now he was glaring at me as if he had detention—or worse—on his mind.

"Yes, Mr. Broadus?" I squeaked.

"Do you have a hall pass?"

"No, sir," I squeaked again.

"Then why aren't you in homeroom?"

"I . . . *am* in homeroom," I blurted out without thinking. It was the truth, though. My double was sitting right in the front row.

Mr. Broadus frowned. "If that's a joke, Mr. Fenton, it isn't funny. I suppose you're late again. Well, you'd better go to the office right now. This is your third tardiness this month, if I'm not mistaken. Tell the attendance officer I recommend detention."

"Yes, sir," I croaked.

I turned and scuttled down the hall toward the school office. But I didn't go inside. Instead, I ducked into the language lab, which, luckily for me, was empty. I stayed there until the first period bell rang. Seconds later, a class of fourth graders came filing into the room.

One of them, a twerpy kid with glasses, stared at me. "What are you doing in here?" he demanded in a high, whiny voice. "You're not in Mr. Whitlock's English class."

"No, I'm not," I said. "In fact, I'm just leaving."

I ran down the hall toward my first-period class. It was Ms. March's history class.

I didn't feel like standing up and talking to the whole

class about the exciting social life of the Pilgrims, but I had no choice. When I got to the door of the classroom, though, something made me stop.

It was that familiar voice again.

"Yes, Ms. March, I'm ready for my presentation," I heard my double say. "I never realized the Pilgrims were so interesting."

"I'm delighted to hear you say that, Chris," Ms. March twittered.

I shuffled down the hall, dragging my feet. *I should feel relieved,* I told myself. *At least now I don't have to talk about the dumb Pilgrims for ten minutes.*

But I didn't feel relieved. I was supposed to be in class, but I couldn't be in class. So where should I go?

In the end, I went into the back stairwell and sat at the top of the stairs for ten minutes or so. I would have sat there all period, except I heard footsteps that sounded suspiciously like Mr. Broadus's. I didn't want to think about what the assistant principal would say—or do!—if he found me in the hall without a pass again!

My heart pounding, I clambered back up to the second floor and ducked into the boys' bathroom. I needed to think fast.

I gazed at my face in the mirror. That was odd. It looked as if there were two of me. But that couldn't be right. I shook my head to clear it and checked again. Two anxious-looking faces stared back at me, and both of them were mine. I stuck out my tongue. Both reflections stuck their tongues out back at me. I groaned loudly. As if things weren't bad enough, now I was losing my mind.

Then one of the reflections smiled and started to laugh.

I spun around. My double was standing right in front of me, a smirk on his face.

"Surprise," he said in a taunting voice.

Chapter 8

"You!" I gasped. "How did you get here?"

My double grinned and flashed a hall pass under my nose. "I have permission to be here," he said. "I saw you run past our classroom and asked Ms. March if I could go to the bathroom. You and I have some things we need to talk about."

"I totally agree," I said, feeling incredibly relieved. "Look, whatever your name is—"

"Chris," my double interrupted with another smirk.

"Chris," I repeated reluctantly.

"Or if you prefer—" My double hesitated, then said something that sounded like *Emmett.*

"Emmett?" I said.

"No, *Emmitt.* It sounds like *time* spelled backward."

"Whatever," I said, losing patience. "Well, look, Emmitt or Chris or whatever you call yourself. I know you've been—um, created to help me and stuff, but you don't need to go to all my classes. I mean, it's a little awkward having two of us, so I guess we should work something out. Like maybe you should go somewhere else or something while I—"

I broke off. I was about to say *while I go to school,* but the funny expression in his eyes stopped me. His eyes—

the same greenish-brown as mine—were shining with a cold, hard light. He looked scary.

"What is it?" I said.

"You just don't get it, do you, Chris?" my double asked.

"Get what?"

He leaned toward me until his nose was almost touching mine. It was like looking into a mirror. "You have to meet your commitments," my double went on in a weird, singsong voice. His voice didn't sound like my voice anymore. It sounded like the voice of a computer come to life. "Time is everything, and you can't afford to lose time."

I was totally baffled. "What are you talking about ?" I asked.

My double threw up his hands. "You couldn't hack it, Chris," he said, his eyes gleaming brighter. "Let's face facts—you were never on time. You were late for everything."

I gulped. There was something about the way he was talking about me in the past tense that gave me the creeps. "So?" I sputtered.

"I am always on time," my double replied smugly. "I'm just like you, only better." He snapped his fingers. "I can do everything you can do, Chris, and more. You needed me, but I don't need you."

"What?" I squawked. I still didn't get it.

He squared his shoulders. "Why don't you just beat it, Chris? Stop following me around. You're making my life too complicated."

"But . . . but what am I supposed do?"

"Whatever you want," my double replied. "Go to the park, go home and watch TV, go shopping . . ."

"But I'm a kid. I have to be at school!" I cried.

My double shrugged. "Not anymore, Chris," he said with a sneer. "Now excuse me, I've got to get back to class." He pushed past me and walked out the door.

I stood there in shock. I couldn't have heard what I thought I'd heard. *Stop following me around. You're making my life too complicated.*

My double was telling me to get lost while he took over my life.

Chapter 9

I clenched my fists. "I can't let him do this!" I muttered. "I can't!" I couldn't believe I'd ever wanted a double. I couldn't believe I'd ever thought having a double would be cool. Then again, I had never really believed it could happen. When I'd clicked on *yes* at the end of the TimeSolvers quiz, I'd never dreamed a computer program could truly make an exact copy of me. I'd thought it was Josh goofing around.

I unclenched my hands. My double might look like me on the outside, but he wasn't me. He was like my evil twin or one of the human slaves in *Alien Invasion from Planet B.*

I started to think hard. If only I knew more about my double—where he'd come from, how he'd been created—maybe I could put a stop to him. Maybe I could even find a way to return him! After all, the Web site had stated *Complete satisfaction guaranteed,* and right now I was one unhappy customer.

One thing was clear: I had to get on-line. Maybe I could get in touch with Professor Chronos through the Internet and talk to him, plead with him to take my double back. It was a long shot, but I couldn't think of anything else to do.

I started toward the bathroom door. Before I got there, the door creaked open. I looked up. It was Mr. Broadus, and he looked mad.

"Chris Fenton," he barked. "Why aren't you in class?"

"I . . . uh—" My throat suddenly closed. I was in big trouble now. Then I spotted a pink slip of paper on the floor. My double must have dropped it. I reached down and scooped it up. "I have a pass!" I whispered.

"Let me see that." Mr. Broadus grabbed the pass out of my hand and squinted at it. "*Humph*. Well, this is a pass, Mr. Fenton, but"—his insect eyes focused on mine—"I think I'll escort you back to class myself. It seems to me you've done enough running around the halls for one morning." Mr. Broadus opened the door and waved me out into the hall. I meekly followed him. What else could I do?

As our footsteps tapped down the hall toward Ms. March's class, my heart began to beat faster and faster. Talk about stress. What was going to happen when Mr. Broadus escorted me into Ms. March's class and found out I was already there?

Whatever happened, it wasn't going to be pretty. Mr. Broadus would probably think it was some kind of practical joke. Unfortunately, though, Mr. Broadus didn't have a good sense of humor. He'd probably give me and my double detention for life!

As we came up to Ms. March's classroom, I broke out in a cold sweat. "Come on, Chris," Mr. Broadus commanded. He pulled the door of the classroom open with a creak. "I've come to deliver one of your students back to you, Ms. March," he boomed. He shoved me into the room.

At that same moment, I felt a cold breeze whip past

me. Before I could figure out what it was, twenty-three pairs of eyes turned to gaze at me. For the first time in my life, I wished I really could meet an alien and be teleported to his distant galaxy. "Uh . . . hi, Ms. March," I fumbled. I was too nervous to even look around for my double.

Ms. March's mouth fell open. "Why, Chris," she said. "How did you get out there? Get back in your seat at once." She pointed to an empty desk at the front of the room. "Thanks, Mr. Broadus," she said vaguely.

Mr. Broadus frowned, but he didn't say anything more. He just waved and stalked out of the room. My legs felt like rubber as I walked up to the place where my double had been sitting earlier.

A notebook lay open on the desk. It had my name on it, but I'd never seen it before.

Nervously, I glanced around. Obviously, my double had just been here, but where was he now? He couldn't have simply vanished into thin air.

As I sat down, my gaze fell on the classroom door. A face with brown hair was looking in at me through the window. *My* face.

I whirled back to look at Ms. March. "Now, after Chris's excellent presentation"—she nodded at me and smiled—"you may be wondering what else there is to know about the Pilgrims. The answer is, a lot."

As Ms. March droned on, I felt my heart start beating fast again. How had my double gotten outside the classroom like that? Maybe he had special powers.

Just then, I noticed Josh giving me a strange look.

"What is it?" I whispered.

"How did you do that?" he whispered back.

"Do what?" I replied.

Ms. March peered at us over the top of her glasses. "Chris, Josh," she said sternly, "how many times do I have to tell you it's rude to whisper when your teacher is talking?"

"Yes, ma'am," I murmured.

"Thank you," said Ms. March. Then she started yakking about the Pilgrims again.

I did my best to settle down and pay attention, but I couldn't. I could tell Josh was having trouble, too. He kept looking at me.

"So how did you do it?" he whispered again.

"Do what?" I asked.

"Disappear like that?" Josh hissed. "And put on a different shirt," he added. "The one you were wearing before had red and blue stripes."

Ms. March gave us another look. "Josh, Chris. What did I tell you?"

"No talking," Josh mumbled.

Ms. March nodded and went on teaching.

I bent over the open notebook on my desk, pretending to take notes, but I wasn't. I couldn't even hear what Ms. March was saying. I was too busy thinking. Josh had noticed that I'd disappeared.

With a sudden flash of inspiration, I turned back a page in the notebook. Now I had more proof that my double had definitely been there. He'd taken comprehensive, well-organized notes—only in my messy handwriting.

I let out a breath. In a way it was a relief to realize I wasn't crazy, but in another way it wasn't. My double was real, and he was determined to take my place.

What was worse, he was better organized than I was. A better student. A better big brother. A better everything.

And he could disappear into thin air anytime he wanted to.

How could I fight someone like that?

Then it came to me. If he had disappeared when I showed up, he must not want to be caught any more than I did. Maybe we both couldn't be in the same place at the same time if there were other people around.

That meant I could get rid of him.

Or at least keep him out of my life.

All I had to do was go to class as if everything were normal and be on time everywhere. A smile slid across my face just as the bell rang.

"Review the chapter on the settlement in Plymouth, Massachusetts for the quiz tomorrow," Ms. March shouted over the noise of kids jumping up from their desks. "And Chris," she said, beaming at me, "that was truly a well-done presentation. I'm so pleased you relate so well to the Pilgrims."

"It wasn't me," I replied softly, but she didn't hear. I leaped to my feet and ran for the door. I had to get to my next class—music—before my double did.

Chapter 10

"**W**ait, Chris!" Josh called after me.

I turned to look back at my best friend. I wanted to tell him everything, but there wasn't enough time. "I can't talk now, Josh," I sputtered. "I've got to get to class on time today!"

Josh screwed up his face and ran to catch up with me. "Chris," he panted. "I'm in your music class, too, remember? What's going on with you anyway?"

I swallowed guiltily. "Look, Josh," I said. "I can't explain now, but I'll tell you soon, I promise."

"Yeah, right," Josh said coldly.

I shook my head. If I didn't tell him, he was going to get mad at me all over again. And this time he probably wouldn't forgive me in a hurry. I took a deep breath. "Okay. Remember that Web site, TimeSolvers, and that quiz I took last night? Well, something's happened, something—"

Suddenly, a hand clamped down on my shoulder.

"That's it, Chris Fenton. You're in big trouble now."

I turned around. It was my archenemy, Mr. Broadus!

I looked up at the assistant principal warily. Out of the corner of my eye, I could see Josh making a sympathetic face.

"What is it, Mr. Broadus?" I said meekly.

"You have some explaining to do, Mr. Fenton."

I licked my lips. "Yes, sir."

"Why didn't you go to the school office to sign in late when I told you to?" Mr. Broadus boomed.

I opened my mouth, but no sound came out. What could I possibly say? *I wasn't late?* The only problem was that Mr. Broadus had seen me outside my homeroom after the bell had rung. "Sir, I—"

"He wasn't late!" Josh piped up indignantly.

Mr. Broadus squinted at him. "What do you know about this, Mr. Burnett?" he growled.

Josh took a step closer to me. "Chris wasn't late," he repeated bravely. "We're in the same homeroom, sir, and he was right on time. He was even a few minutes early. You can ask Ms. Nelson!"

Mr. Broadus looked at me and then at Josh. "I'll do just that," he said severely. "But something strange is going on here."

"Mr. Broadus, is there a problem?"

I whirled around, and then I smiled. It was Mr. Delgado. As usual, he was wearing a crazy tie. This one had fluorescent numbers splashed all over it.

"I'm not sure yet," Mr. Broadus replied, an ominous look on his face.

"Well, I'd better take Chris with me if you're through with him. He's due in my band class in five minutes, and you know Chris—he has a tendency to be late," Mr. Delgado said smoothly.

"Uh, yes," Mr. Broadus muttered awkwardly. Then he flashed me a look that said, *You haven't heard the last of this.*

I didn't care. I was too relieved. Mr. Delgado had

come to my rescue, which meant he mustn't be mad anymore.

"It's great you showed up, Mr. Delgado," Josh said. "Now we'll all make it to class on time."

Mr. Delgado scowled. "Sure. Umm . . . Josh," he said slowly, "why don't you go on ahead? I have a private matter to discuss with Chris."

Josh looked confused for a moment. "All right. See you."

"See you in class, Josh," Mr. Delgado said warmly. Then he looked down at me, a sympathetic expression in his eyes. "Well, well, Chris," he said cheerfully. "Mr. Broadus sure seems to have it in for you. What was he so upset about?"

"Oh," I replied with a shrug, "he thought I was somewhere I shouldn't be this morning, but I wasn't."

Mr. Delgado shot me a strange look. I couldn't blame him. My explanation didn't make a lot of sense, but if I told him the truth, he'd think I was really weird.

I cleared my throat. "So what did you want to talk to me about?" I asked nervously. I figured it was about me being late for band practice yesterday, or maybe it was something about my playing. *Whatever it is, it isn't good,* I thought, my heart sinking.

Mr. Delgado's eyes gleamed at me from behind his glasses. "I don't want to talk about this in the hall," he said pleasantly. "Come on. We can have a nice, quiet talk in here." He led me into a classroom and shut the door behind him.

I blinked and looked around. We were in the computer lab. "Hey, Mr. Delgado," I said. "Why did—?" I was about to say, *Why did you bring me in here?* when my jaw dropped open. Sitting at the computer terminal in the far corner was my double. He lifted his head and looked at me disdainfully.

"Is everything ready?" Mr. Delgado asked Emmitt.

"Yup," my double replied. "Ready and waiting!"

Chapter 11

I gaped at Mr. Delgado. "You know about him?" I said in a strangled voice as I gestured at my double.

Mr. Delgado just smiled. I looked into his eyes. Normally they were brown, twinkly eyes—friendly eyes—but now they shone with a cold, bluish light. In an instant it came to me. The reason Mr. Delgado had acted so weird and stern the day before was that he wasn't really Mr. Delgado. It had been his double, just like the boy in front of the computer screen wasn't really me, but my evil twin!

I took a step backward. "You're not Mr. Delgado, are you?" I whispered in horror. "You're—" My voice trailed off. The man was coming toward me fast. I took another step backward and slammed my leg into the corner of a desk.

"Ouch!" I tried to move, but I wasn't fast enough. The fake Mr. Delgado grabbed hold of me. He started pulling me toward the computer at the far end of the room. Out of the corner of my eye, I saw that my double was typing something on the keyboard.

"Hey," I yelped. "What's going on?"

The man's eyes bored into mine. "You wouldn't cooperate, Chris," he said softly. He pointed at my double. "He told you to make yourself scarce, but you wouldn't listen."

"Of course I wouldn't listen!" I protested. "It's my life!"

"*Was* your life," the fake Mr. Delgado corrected me. "But you weren't honoring your commitments, Chris. Time is everything. You can't afford to waste time."

My double nodded, repeating the same words in that eerie singsong voice. "Time is everything. We can't afford to waste time," they both chanted.

I looked from one clone to the other. I had to make a run for it—now! I sucked in my breath and kicked the fake Mr. Delgado in the left shin. He let out a gasp of pain and tightened his grip on my arm.

"Start up the reverse function," he ordered in a grim voice.

My double punched some commands into the computer. Even from across the room, I recognized the graphics on the screen. They were from the home page of the TimeSolvers Web site.

Mr. Delgado dragged me across the room and pushed me into a seat right in front of the computer. I didn't know what was going to happen next, but I knew that whatever it was, it wasn't going to be pleasant. "Let me go!" I pleaded.

My evil double leaned over me. "Bye, Chris," he said. "Nice knowing you." He pressed another button on the keyboard.

"No," I screamed. "Please, don't!"

As I struggled, I heard a door open behind me. "Mr. Delgado? Chris?" a familiar voice called. "Are you two—?"

I twisted my head around. Josh was standing in the doorway. "Get help, Josh!" I shouted.

But it was too late. Josh had spotted my double. His eyes widened, and he took a step inside. "Hey, Chris, what's going on?" he demanded, looking baffled.

My double didn't hesitate. He ran forward and grabbed Josh by the shoulders. Josh was too surprised to put up much of a fight. Besides, Josh is sort of a shrimp, so he didn't have a chance. I would have helped him if I could, but the fake Mr. Delgado was holding me pinned to my seat. Later, I thought maybe I should have shouted for help, but it all happened too fast.

In seconds Josh was beside me, and the two of us were directly in front of the brightly lit computer screen. "Press the button, Emmitt," my double said to the fake Mr. Delgado.

"Yes, Emmitt," the fake Mr. Delgado replied. I heard the click of his finger on the keyboard, and a white-hot light came flashing out of the monitor. The light was so bright, it felt as if my eyes were on fire. I tried to turn toward Josh, but I couldn't move.

That was when I looked down and realized what was happening. I was disappearing! I wanted to scream, but no sound came out of my mouth. First my sneakers vanished, then my ankles, then my knees. I felt as if I had pins and needles all over. "Help!" I tried to shout again. Then the light grew brighter, and I couldn't see anything anymore.

Chapter 12

When I opened my eyes, I thought for a moment it was night and I was in a parking lot. Bright green, yellow, and red lights were shining all around. They looked like car headlights, but they were coming from all directions. I tried to stand up, but my body felt strange—sort of rubbery and wobbly.

"Josh," I shouted hoarsely. "Where are you?"

"Over here," came Josh's voice. He sounded scared. "Hey, Chris, do you notice anything strange?"

"Everything—" I started to reply. Then I glanced down at my feet and let out a cry. They looked like my feet—that is, I still had white basketball shoes with red laces and white socks on—but up close, my shoes and socks appeared to be made of zillions of tiny dots.

"What in the world . . .?" I gasped. I stretched out my hands and stared at them. I wiggled my fingers. No wonder I felt strange and rubbery. My hands, my feet, my whole body had been turned into a bunch of dots. I was a walking cartoon!

"Josh, where are you?" I repeated.

"Over here," Josh replied. I whirled around. It was Josh, all right. Not too tall, curly dark hair, thick glasses, some freckles. But it was as if someone had taken the flesh-and-blood Josh I knew and made him into a computer drawing.

"I don't believe this," I shrieked. "We've been turned into Saturday morning cartoons!"

"Not cartoons," Josh corrected me. "We're computer animations. Some high-powered computers can scan things and instantly come up with computer images of them. I read about it in the latest issue of *CompuWorld*. I'm pretty sure that's what's happened to us, but I don't know how."

I shook my head. In one way I was relieved that Josh was so calm, but it really bugged me too. *Only a true computer geek would talk about technology at a time like this,* I thought crossly.

"I don't think the technology really matters," I said aloud. "Something weird is going on. Who did this to us?"

But Josh paid no attention. "The really amazing thing is that we still have voices," he continued. "I can't figure out how the programmers—"

"Josh!" I yelled. "Cut it out! I know you're interested in this stuff, but what's happened to us isn't just technology gone wrong. It's—"

I broke off when I saw Josh's face. He looked as if he was about to cry. "I know," he said. "I knew when I saw two of you in the computer lab that something bad had happened. It was that quiz you took, right? That TimeSolvers thing? When the computer said it had copied you, it was telling the truth, wasn't it, Chris?"

"Yeah," I replied miserably. "It copied me physically, all right, but it wasn't how I thought it would be. It's like I woke up and discovered I had an evil twin. At first, I

58

thought having a double might be sort of cool, you know? I thought he could help me get stuff done. But my double wasn't anything like me. He just wanted to take over my life, and—"

"Now he has," Josh interrupted softly.

The way he said it made me feel incredibly guilty. Thanks to me, Josh had been sucked into this bizarre place. I turned away and began to study the flashing lights again, trying to figure out where we were. Then I saw that the lights were actually letters. I squinted, trying to read what they said. *Exit document? Yes/No,* I read slowly. My heart started pounding as I realized what had happened.

The doubles had zapped us into a computer. Josh and I were now part of a computer program.

I wondered if Josh had already figured that part out. "Hey, Josh, am I totally nuts, or are we inside a computer?"

Josh let out a long, shuddering sigh. "I think so, Chris. I don't know how it could have happened, but we're animated computer figures. We seem to be part of a Web site."

"But . . ." I swallowed around the big lump in my throat. "How do we get out?"

Josh looked at me and shook his head. "I haven't a clue," he said. "I know a lot about computers, but I don't know anything about being part of one."

"Great," I replied. "Well, I guess we'd better do some exploring."

"Exploring? Where?" Josh asked.

"I don't know. Let's try this way." I pointed to where the lights were shining brightest, hoping there would be something that would help us figure out how to get out.

I started toward the lights. When I turned to see if Josh was following me, I couldn't see him anywhere.

"Josh?" I shouted. "Josh, where are you?"

But there was no answer. Josh had vanished into thin air.

Chapter 13

"Josh, come on! Where are you?" I pleaded. I felt a prickly pins-and-needles feeling spread all over me. Being stuck in a computer was bad enough, but being trapped in one alone was more than I could take. "Please, Josh, answer me!"

I heard a snicker beside me, and then a flash of color like a quick-moving rainbow danced in front of my eyes. Slowly, the rainbow turned into Josh.

"Josh! Where did you go?" I cried. I'd never been as happy to see anyone in my life.

"Hey, I was right!" Josh said.

"Right about what?" I couldn't believe he'd disappeared like that on purpose.

"Well, like most computer animation, we're only two-dimensional," Josh explained eagerly. "Sure, we look three-dimensional, but we're not. So I figured if I turned sideways fast enough, I'd disappear, and I was right!"

"Terrific," I said grumpily. "Don't do that again, okay?"

Josh's smile faded. "Sorry," he said. "But you never know—information like that might be useful. It might even help us get out of here."

"I doubt it," I retorted.

Then I remembered how my double had appeared and disappeared. Maybe that was how he'd done it. He'd probably spun around and around to keep out of sight. That could even explain the breeze I'd felt as I went into Ms. March's classroom. But if that was true, then my double wasn't real. He was just a walking computer image, like me. Or was he?

I put the question out of my mind and forced myself to concentrate on getting us out of there. I peered around in the darkness. "We'd better keep looking for a way out," I told Josh.

"But where?" Josh said nervously. "Everywhere I look, it's the same—all those bright lights. Who knows what might be out there?"

"True," I agreed. "But I don't think we're the only ones stuck in here." I explained to him quickly about the fake Mr. Delgado. "He was in on it with my double," I said, "which means that he isn't the real Mr. Delgado. And if he's a clone, then the real Mr. Delgado must be somewhere else—maybe even in here with us."

"Good point," Josh said. "But which way should we go? Every place looks the same to me—empty."

"I'm not sure," I admitted, looking around again. I walked forward cautiously and bumped against something hard. *Great,* I thought, *not only are we trapped inside a computer, but there are walls in here. We're probably locked in a little box and we don't even know it!*

Then I heard Josh yell, "Chris, over here! I've found something."

I turned around. My eyes were slowly adjusting to the bright lights, because for the first time I could make out dim shapes around us—squares and rectangles, like a city a kid might make out of cardboard boxes. But I couldn't see Josh.

"Up here!" he called.

I looked up. Josh was standing on top of a big, square shape—some kind of raised platform. I scrambled toward him. The platform was higher than my head.

"Hey, how did you get up there?" I called.

Josh chuckled. "I flew," he said.

"You what?" I snarled.

"I flew. Give it a try. Just jump and flap your arms."

I did. To my amazement, it did feel like flying. I was rising through the air, and as long as I kept my arms moving, I kept rising higher and higher.

"Hey, I can fly!" I shouted, like Peter Pan.

Josh and I grinned at each other for a moment. Then, as I landed next to him with a soft thump, we both grew serious again. It was great to fly, but it would have been better if we were ourselves instead of part of some computer program.

"What is this?" I asked, looking down at my feet. The square platform was made up of lots of little squares all stuck together, sort of like a keyboard on a typewriter. On each square were raised letters and numbers.

"F1, F2, F3," I read aloud. "I don't get it. What do these numbers and letters mean?" I squinted down at the platform. It looked like some kind of weird hopscotch board or a giant game of some kind.

Josh leaned toward me. "It's a computer template," he explained. "These are all function keys. We were right. Somehow we've been transported into a computer program, and what we're standing on is the function center." He looked down at his feet. "Now, if I can just make these keys work, maybe we can do something about getting out of here."

He jumped hard on a square that said *F3*.

Instantly, a giant sign lit up over our heads. *F3: Help.* In smaller letters below, it read, *Press any function key to get information about the use of the key.*

Josh jumped again. Ribbons of letters scrolled through the air. *F1: This key will set up your document and, used in combination with the Ctrl key, allows you to retrieve program memory. To use . . .* I read on, and then I groaned. "Terrific," I said. "I've never understood computers, and now I'm part of one."

"It's not that hard to understand," Josh replied. "In fact, it's actually pretty interesting."

I stared at him. He sounded as if he were glad we were inside this program. Didn't he understand how much trouble we were in?

"See, like I was telling you," Josh continued, "this platform is the program template. It's where all the function keys are located. If we use it right, we can figure out where we are and what the program does. Then we can work on getting back to the real world."

He jumped on another key. *Location* flashed above. *Page 1 of document.*

"A-ha," Josh said. "So we're at the first page of the document. That explains why you bumped into a wall over there. You must have hit the page break. See this key down here—*Page Down*? I bet if we push it, we'll go to the next page of the document."

"How about pushing *Exit* instead, so we can get out of here?" I suggested.

"Chris, that's a great idea!" Josh cried. He started to run to the far end of the template.

I ran after him. "Josh, where are you going?"

"F7 is the exit function, Chris," he replied. "If I jump on the key hard enough, maybe we *can* get out!"

"Yeah, but where will we go?" I demanded. I had a sudden picture of us just vanishing. Bad as it was being where we were, just disappearing into nothingness seemed worse.

Josh stopped and thought for a moment. "Well, we might end up in DOS."

"What's DOS?" I asked.

"The computer disk operating system."

"Huh?"

Josh took a deep breath. I could tell he was about to explain it in a lot more detail.

"Never mind," I cut in fast. "Maybe jumping on F7 isn't such a good idea after all. I think we'd better stay here until we know more about what's going on."

Josh's cartoon eyes blinked. "You're probably right," he whispered. We looked at each other. "I'm scared, Chris," he blurted.

I had to agree with Josh. In fact, I was terrified. Before I could say as much, I saw new letters flash over our heads. I was standing on the key labeled *F10,* and I must have landed on it hard enough to set it off. *MemoryFile retrieved,* the letters read. Beneath the words, just a few feet away from us, was something outlined in blue light. It looked like a door.

Cautiously, I inched forward. It *was* a door! And it was open—just a crack.

I lifted my hand to touch the letters on the door. They were in the same style as the letters on the squares of the template. *MemoryFile,* I read silently. I stretched out my arm and gently pushed the door open.

"I don't want to go in there," Josh squeaked.

"We've got to go in," I hissed back. "This is the first break we've had! Maybe this door is our only way out of this place!"

Josh didn't say anything, so I pushed the door open the rest of the way and stepped inside.

The whole place shone with a bright blue light. I blinked and rubbed my cartoon eyes with my cartoon fists. I couldn't figure out where all the light was coming from. The room appeared to be a long hallway, like a gallery in a museum. On both sides of the hallway were rectangular shapes that looked like boxes. I did a double take as I realized what was inside them—statues of people!

"Whoa . . ." Josh breathed.

I peered more closely at the boxes. The people weren't exactly statues. They were cartoon figures—life-size, two-dimensional graphics of people. Some were kids like me, and some were grown-ups. All of them were perfectly lifeless. Then I noticed something that made my skin crawl. The boxes containing the people were shaped just like coffins!

I cautiously stepped up to one of the boxes and studied the figure inside. It was an old man in a crisp white suit.

I sucked in my breath. The old man was Professor Chronos!

On the top edge of the box was a plaque with a name on it. *Chronos, Professor Peter,* I read. I took a quick step backward. "Hey, Josh," I called softly.

"Chris, look at this," I heard Josh whisper behind me. He sounded very scared.

I turned around and looked into the box in front of

Josh. The statue inside was someone I knew well—Mr. Delgado.

"He's dead!" Josh babbled. "I touched him, and he didn't move! It's Mr. Delgado, and he's dead!"

We looked at each other in horror. Then I noticed something even more terrifying. The box next to Mr. Delgado's was empty, and the plaque on the top of it said, *Fenton, Chris!*

Chapter 14

My jaw dropped. If I weren't a cartoon, the hair on my head probably would have stood up or I would have broken out in goose bumps. Instead, I started to get that funny pins-and-needles feeling again. Then I saw Josh examining another empty box closer to the door.

"'Josh Burnett'!" he shouted. "This one's for me!" He ran up and grabbed my arm. "Come on, Chris! Let's get out of here!"

I didn't argue. The two of us turned and headed for the door. We raced down the long, blue-lit hallway into the main template and slammed the door tight behind us.

"The doubles must have killed Mr. Delgado and put him there," Josh stammered, his eyes wide.

My head was spinning. This was just like *Alien Invasion from Planet B*. I wondered if the doubles were aliens trying to take over our bodies and conquer the earth.

I gazed at the place where the door had been. It wasn't lit up anymore, but I thought I could see the faint outlines of the letters in the darkness. *MemoryFile. Why is it called that?* I wondered. If Mr. Delgado and Professor

Chronos were dead, why did the doubles keep computer likenesses of them on file?

I shook my head. There was so much about this I didn't understand. I had a bad feeling that if I didn't figure things out fast, it would be too late.

"What do we do now?" Josh asked.

"I don't know," I started to say. "Maybe we should hide—" As I spoke, I heard something. It was a click like a light switch being turned on—only much louder. Seconds later a bright blue light surrounded us. It was like the light in the MemoryFile room, only a thousand times stronger. I lifted my hands to shield my eyes. Then I squinted and glanced around.

The space in front of me was glowing like a giant window.

I tried to run, but I couldn't. I was paralyzed.

"Josh," I tried to shout, but no sound came out.

By concentrating, I managed to swivel my eyes in Josh's direction. What I saw made me feel even worse.

Josh was paralyzed, too, and for some reason, his mouth was turned up in a stupid grin. Letters flashed in front of our eyes. *Welcome to the TimeSolvers Web site! If time management is a problem for you, just take our simple TimeSolvers quiz. In a few minutes, you'll be on your way to solving your scheduling problems forever!*

I felt the corners of my mouth turn up. I tried to stop smiling, but I couldn't move my lips, so I just stood there grinning like an idiot. My eyes were getting used to the light, though. As I stared straight ahead, I realized I was looking through a window—a huge window of thick, curved glass. Figures were moving behind it, giant blobs the size of dinosaurs. Then one of the blobs came closer, and I saw it was a person. I couldn't see too clearly, but I could tell that the giant was coming closer and closer. Its enormous arms were reaching out toward the window, and there was nothing I could do to stop it.

Chapter 15

"Hey, that's odd," a girl's voice said. The voice sounded as if it were coming from far away. It sounded familiar, too. The huge blob settled down in the front of the window. I stared in shock. If I could have moved, I think I would have jumped out of my skin.

Staring in at me from the other side of the window was a giant face—and it belonged to Jenna!

"Someone must have left this computer on and just turned the monitor off," the giant Jenna exclaimed. "It looks like it's on some kind of game."

"What?" another voice said. That voice sounded familiar, too, but I couldn't identify it.

Jenna didn't answer. She just leaned closer. Her face looked a little blurry through the curved glass, but I saw her eyebrows suddenly shoot up.

"TimeSolvers!" she breathed. "Too strange. Someone must have left this computer on-line. But why couldn't I find the TimeSolvers Web site yesterday?" Then she squinted at Josh and me. "Weird," she said. "These little cartoon figures look just like you and Chris."

Another face came into view. I was horrified. It was Josh's face—a giant Josh. I wished I could turn my head to see my friend's reaction.

I knew I had a double, but how had Josh gotten one? Could the TimeSolvers page have copied him at the same time it was sucking him inside? I watched in dread as the giant Josh face came closer. Its eyes were green and round just like my friend's, but they had the same cold expression as the eyes of my double.

"Jenna, you're crazy. They're just two cartoon kids. They don't look anything like me or Chris," the fake Josh said smoothly, his giant lips forming each word carefully.

"Look! They're even wearing your clothes!"

"So? Most kids wear jeans and T-shirts. They're just cartoons."

"Two cartoons that look exactly like you and Chris." Jenna's voice rose. "And check out this site—TimeSolvers. It's the same Web site—"

"Jenna, you'd better just exit out of there. We have work to do, remember?" The fake Josh's voice sounded angry.

I raised my eyes. Whatever force was keeping us paralyzed was weakening. Concentrating as hard as I could, I looked down. I was standing on the F3 key. If I could move my feet just a little, I might be able to send Jenna a message!

I focused all my energy on moving my feet. At first, nothing happened, but finally I managed to shuffle one foot and then the other. I didn't move that much, but it was enough. I felt like cheering as the word *Help* flashed up onto the screen.

Jenna frowned. "That's strange," she murmured. "The screen is flashing *Help* at me."

"Jenna, you're losing it," the fake Josh said impatiently. "Hurry up and get out of there."

Just then a third head came into view. "Kids, what's

going on here?" It was our computer teacher, Mr. Murray. Fifth period was computer lab for fifth and sixth graders.

"I don't know, Mr. Murray. When I turned on the monitor, this Web site came up on the screen," Jenna explained.

"TimeSolvers," read Mr. Murray. "It sounds like a game. Well, Jenna, you know we're not supposed to play games during computer class. Today we're going to work on learning the BASIC programming language. Now click on *Exit* and get out of there at once."

"But—"

Before Jenna could say anything more, Josh's hand flashed across the screen. I felt everything tilting, just as if I were riding on a Ferris wheel—faster, faster. A blur passed in front of my eyes. In the blur I could see the fake Josh grinning at me evilly.

Suddenly I felt myself falling. The weird pins-and-needles feeling had come back, but this time it was much stronger than it had been before—so strong that I felt like I was dissolving. Then something exploded inside my head, and I passed out.

Chapter 16

"Chris, wake up!"

Someone was shouting and shaking me back and forth like a rag doll. Groggily, I opened my eyes. I expected to see Josh, but instead, an old man was leaning over me—an old man with glasses and a white suit.

Professor Chronos.

"You," I gasped. I saw that I was standing in a coffin-shaped box. I was in the MemoryFile. I jumped out of my box. And then I saw Josh. He was standing in the box with his name written over it, and he was completely motionless. I prayed he would move, but he didn't.

He looked as dead as a cartoon could look.

I whirled around and glared at the professor. I felt like punching him. This whole thing was his fault. "What did you do to him?" I shouted.

Professor Chronos sighed. "I didn't do anything," he said softly.

"Yes, you did!" I yelled. "You turned us both into computer-animated cartoons, and then you killed him!"

The professor put up his hands. "Calm down, young man! First of all, your friend isn't dead. He's just being read."

"Being read?" I repeated.

74

The professor nodded. "Josh's double is scanning his mind for information," he said solemnly. "That's the only way the doubles can function in the real world." The professor sighed again. "We can't function when we're being read," he added sorrowfully. "That's why none of us have managed to put a stop to him," he whispered.

I was confused. "Put a stop to whom?" I cried.

"Emmitt," the professor replied.

"Emmitt?" I muttered. Then I remembered: *Emmitt* was what my double had called himself when I'd asked him his name. It was also the name of Mr. Delgado's double.

"Who is this Emmitt guy?" I asked. But the pins-and-needles feeling was starting to come back again. I noticed that my hands were becoming transparent. Then I looked over at the box with my name on it.

Oh, no! I thought. There I could see a faint outline of myself!

I was starting to feel sleepy—very, very sleepy. The professor grabbed me by the arm and shook me hard. "Hey," I protested weakly.

"Your double is starting to read you again," he said urgently. "But you can't go to sleep. You can't let him make you lose consciousness. Force yourself to stay awake, boy. You have to listen to what I'm going to tell you." His voice sounded distant, like a voice in a dream. All I could think about was closing my eyes, but I struggled to stay awake.

"I was trying to build the first computer that would think like a person," the professor was saying. "Emmitt was my lab assistant, and in many ways he was a far more brilliant scientist than I was. He convinced me that a computer could never think like a person until it had a body. He said that to make a computer as intelligent as a person, I needed to take over a person's mind with a computer."

"Take over a person's mind with a computer?" I repeated hazily. "Is that what's going on?"

Professor Chronos took off his glasses and rubbed his eyes. "Emmitt said that if I helped him, he could become the first computer-person. He would combine the logical intelligence of a computer and the learned intelligence of a human being. All I had to do was invent a computer chip that could be implanted in his brain to read his memory."

I yawned, struggling to follow along. Then I began to wonder if the professor was telling me the truth. Maybe he was just trying to fool me. After all, he was the one who'd gotten me to take the quiz. Feeling more awake, I stared up at the professor. He *looked* honest, but was he?

"I finally made the perfect chip and implanted it in Emmitt's brain," the professor continued. "Then I programmed his memory onto my master computer. Initially I was delighted, because for the first time I had a computer that could think like a human being. Then Emmitt disappeared."

"Where'd he go?" I asked.

Professor Chronos stared at me. "My lab assistant had somehow put himself into the program. Soon afterward, I found out that Emmitt didn't really want to help me create a computer that could think. He wanted to turn himself into a computer program—a program capable of taking over the bodies of all the people of the world. That way, he could live forever."

This can't be real, I thought. There was no way someone could turn into a computer program and take over people's bodies. I looked at Professor Chronos warily. Was he crazy?

"That's an incredible story," I said aloud. "But why should I believe you? You and your stupid quiz got me into this mess."

"It wasn't me," the professor said flatly. "Don't you see? We all have doubles. I admit I should have known better than to trust Emmitt in the first place, but I didn't. By the time I understood his plan, it was too late," he sighed. "The real Emmitt was gone, and in his place was the strongest artificial intelligence ever created. Emmitt now had the power to copy himself over and over again, to take over the minds and bodies of innocent people. I was his first victim."

"You mean all that TimeSolvers stuff on TV wasn't you?" I muttered sleepily. It felt like my mouth was full of molasses.

"No," the professor said, "it was my double. I tried to warn you, but—"

"Warn me? You mean *you* were the one who sent me that e-mail message to beware?" I cried out.

Professor Chronos nodded sadly. "Yes, but Emmitt found out. He punished me. He punished all of us." The professor shuddered. "Somehow he must be stopped!"

Now I believed the professor was telling the truth. No one could make himself look that scared unless he really was. "B-But how?" I stuttered.

"I'm not sure. Emmitt has translated himself into the TimeSolvers computer program. Perhaps if his memory file were erased, that would be the end of him. The name on his file is *Ttimme,* with two *T*s and two *M*s." The professor smiled grimly. "Get it? *Emmitt* in reverse." Then he became serious again. "But if he's erased, I'm not sure the rest of us will ever be able to escape."

As I struggled to take in what the professor was saying, I heard a loud click. The door to the MemoryFile room creaked open. The blue light around us grew brighter.

My heart in my mouth, I lifted my head. Through the open MemoryFile door, I could see a giant version of my own face peering in at us from the other side of the huge curved glass window of the computer screen. The face smiled—a cruel-looking smile. "I hope you two had a nice talk," the face said in a voice that sounded like mine but wasn't. "Because it's probably the last time you'll ever meet!"

I opened my mouth and tried to say something—anything—in response, but the pins-and-needles feeling was getting worse. It felt like tiny electric shocks all over my body. I stared at my double's giant face, but something was happening to my eyes. Everything was getting blurry. I struggled to focus, but it was no use. The world turned black, and I slid into unconsciousness.

Chapter 17

"**C**hris, open your eyes. Please! Please!"

I opened my eyes. I was lying flat on my back, and Josh was leaning over me. His cartoon face looked scared and anxious. "Josh?" I said.

"You're alive," he breathed.

"Yeah, I'm alive." I sat up. I wasn't in the MemoryFile room anymore. Instead, I was lying on the high platform with the function keys—the template, as Josh called it.

I blinked. "How'd I get out here?"

"I dragged you out here!" Josh said with a shudder. "I woke up in that MemoryFile. I was in one of the boxes, and then I saw you. You were in a box, too, and you were just standing there like a statue." Josh shook his head. "I thought you were dead, like Mr. Delgado and that professor guy and all the other people in there."

I rose to my feet. The pins-and-needles feeling was gone. I felt normal—or as normal as a cartoon could feel. "They're not actually dead," I said. "They're just being read."

"Being what?" Josh asked.

I quickly repeated everything the professor had told me—everything I could remember, anyway. It sounded pretty crazy, even to me. I figured Josh would never believe it, but when I was done, he just nodded thoughtfully.

"That Emmitt guy must be a genius," he said soberly. "The question is, what are we going to do about him?"

"You're asking the wrong person," I told him glumly as I recalled the evil smile on my double's face. "I can barely turn my computer on." I looked at Josh. "Couldn't you figure out a way to erase his memory file, like the professor said?"

"If I were outside, I could do it in two seconds," Josh replied. "But stuck in here, I don't think there's a lot I can do."

My heart sank. All along I'd been counting on Josh, the computer whiz, to get us out of this mess.

At that very moment a whoosh of color appeared beside us. Slowly, a cartoon of a middle-aged woman materialized. "Oh!" she said when she saw us. Her hands flew up to her mouth. Then she shook her head. "Oh, dear," she said. "You're new. Who are you?"

"Josh and Chris," Josh answered. "Who are you?"

"I'm Ms. Jenkins, Professor Chronos's secretary," the woman informed us unhappily. "Well, I *was* Professor Chronos's secretary."

"Then maybe you can help us figure out how to get out of here," Josh said eagerly.

But Ms. Jenkins only shook her head. "I wish I could," she replied softly. "But Emmitt is very clever—so clever that I'm afraid we're all helpless, unless . . ." Her voice trailed off.

"Unless what?" Josh shouted.

Ms. Jenkins said something. It sounded like *someone from outside,* but it was hard to tell, because Ms. Jenkins was vanishing. We watched in dismay as she turned into a pattern of brightly colored dots and then faded.

"I guess she's being read again," I said gloomily.

"Great," Josh moaned. "No wonder no one's managed to get out of here. They're being read all the time. Anyway, she didn't tell me anything I don't know. Of course we need outsider help, but how are we ever going to make someone out there understand what's going on in here?"

I didn't know the answer.

Suddenly I heard the click of the giant switch. The space around us became flooded with the bright blue light. I gazed up at the screen in fear. Then my heart lifted.

It was Jenna!

Chapter 18

Jenna gazed at Josh and me, a sad, puzzled look on her face. I longed to shout to her, but I was paralyzed again. I stood there helplessly as the TimeSolvers logo flashed in front of my eyes. If only I could move just a little. I puffed out my cheeks and concentrated as hard as I could. Bit by bit, I lifted my arm.

Then I waved, just a little. Beside me, Josh was doing the same thing.

Jenna watched us, but it was obvious she had no idea why we were waving. All she saw were two tiny computer-animated figures who happened to look like Josh and Chris waving their tiny cartoon arms.

"Jenna! Jenna!" Josh called. His voice sounded high and shrill, and I knew it must be hard for him to talk, but somehow he was doing it. "Jenna, it's me, Josh."

Jenna just stared at us, the same sad expression on her face. She couldn't hear a word Josh was saying.

After a moment, she sighed. "I wish I knew what was going on," she murmured softly. "Because something definitely is. Josh isn't acting anything like himself, and neither is Chris. And I'm probably going crazy, but I keep wondering why you two look so much like them."

"Jenna, it's us. Don't you understand? It's us!" Josh

shouted. But it was plain from Jenna's expression that she didn't even know we were talking to her.

"Forget it," I said. My voice sounded sort of rusty, but at least I could talk. I didn't know why, but I didn't feel as paralyzed as I had the first time Jenna had switched on the computer and found us. "She doesn't know what we're saying. It's hopeless."

Suddenly, Josh let out an excited gasp. "But we're standing on the template," he declared.

"What?" I said.

"The template!" Josh repeated, urgently. "We can try to talk to her with the template again. What key are you standing on?"

I glanced down. "F3 again," I replied. *"Help."* A note of triumph crept into my voice.

"You've got to make it work this time!" Josh's voice was anxious.

"I'll try," I said. I concentrated. Lifting my foot seemed to take every ounce of will I had. Slowly, I raised my foot and brought it down.

Help flashed across the screen.

A wrinkle creased Jenna's forehead. "Help," she read. "What do you mean, 'Help'?"

Help Help Help, I flashed at her. The more I moved, the easier it became. Soon I was jumping up and down on the F3 key.

Jenna watched me in amazement: a tiny cartoon figure jumping up and down in place. "Help?" she breathed. A gleam came into her eyes. "Do you mean you want me to help you?"

Josh and I nodded as hard we could.

Jenna's hand flew up to her mouth and she gasped. "Do you mean you really are . . . Josh and Chris?"

We nodded again even harder. Moving didn't seem nearly so difficult now, and I started to feel more hopeful about getting rescued.

"I don't believe it!" Jenna moaned. "You're really Josh and Chris? But how can I help you? Tell me how!"

Josh and I looked at each other. We didn't know the answer. I thought wildly of what the professor had said. *Erase the memory file* Ttimme.

I turned to Josh. "We have to tell her to erase Emmitt. I mean, *Ttimme*. Can we tell her that?"

"I don't know. We could try. It should be a subfile in the MemoryFile," Josh said.

He ran to a button at the far end of the template. He jumped up and down on it. *Delete file?* flashed up on the screen.

Jenna's face scrunched up in concentration. "You want me to delete the file?" she asked. "The whole thing?"

Josh and I shook our heads vigorously. We certainly didn't want her to delete us!

"So what do you want me to do?"

Josh jumped on function key F4. The words *Create subfile?* appeared on the screen.

"Create subfile," Jenna read out loud. "I don't get it. Do you want me to delete this file or create a new file?"

This was harder than Josh and I had expected. Then Josh had an idea. He pressed the delete button again, then the F4 button again. Now, above our heads, it read: *Delete file? Create subfile?*

Josh pointed up at the word *Delete* while I pointed at the word *subfile*.

Jenna pursed her lips, then she smiled. "Oh, I get it," she said. "You want me to delete a subfile. Cool. Which one?"

Josh and I surveyed the function keys on the

template. I didn't even know what they all did, but Josh knew. "Isn't there one that has the word *time* in it?" I exclaimed frantically.

Josh shook his head. "No." He turned and looked up at Jenna. "Time," he mouthed. "Time! Time! Time!"

But Jenna didn't understand.

We were both getting desperate when Josh yelled, "I've got it! Jump on F1, Chris!" As I did, I saw Josh jump on another key, *Alt*. The words *Set up clock* lit up in the corner of the screen. Josh flashed me a grin. I now saw what he was trying to do and smiled back. But Jenna still looked confused.

I gestured frantically at the word *clock*.

"Delete subfile *Clock*?" Jenna asked, frowning.

Josh and I shook our heads. Then I remembered the games of charades my mom used to play with us, and I made the sign for *like*. Josh made it, too. "Like clock! Like clock!" we signed over and over.

Luckily, Jenna had played charades before. Otherwise I don't think we would ever have gotten our point across. Her face lit up. "Like *clock*," she said. "Okay, what is it? *Minutes? Hours? Time?*"

Bingo. Josh and I both nodded again, smiling encouragement.

"Erase subfile *Time*. Okay, I'll go to the list of subfiles," Jenna murmured. She pressed a function key to list the files in the program, and a list of names and numbers scrolled in front of our eyes. Jenna ran a huge finger down it.

"The only *Time* here has two *T*s and two *M*s," she said thoughtfully. "*Ttimme?* Is that the file you mean?"

We were about to nod again when we heard a loud noise. It sounded like a tree falling, but it wasn't. It was a door opening and closing. Josh and I froze as another face came into view. It was a very familiar face—especially to Josh.

"Hey, Jenna," the face said. "What are you doing?"

Josh and I didn't dare look at each other.

"Nothing, Josh," replied Jenna. Her voice shook a little. "Just checking out something for my computer class."

"I thought I told you never to use my computer without asking," we heard the fake Josh say. His face came a step closer.

"Sorry. I'm just shutting it down," Jenna squeaked.

She reached her fingers toward the Exit button as fast as she could, but it wasn't fast enough. At the same time we heard the sound of the Exit key being depressed, the fake Josh saw us.

Chapter 19

The fake Josh's eyes narrowed, and his mouth turned down at the corners. "Jenna—" we heard him say in a nasty voice. At that moment, the screen went black. Josh and I were left in the darkness. We were both thinking the same thing. *What now?*

At that moment, I heard a voice calling my name. "Chris, is that you? Josh? What are you doing here?"

I whirled around. The door to the MemoryFile was open, and Mr. Delgado was standing there. Mr. Delgado had finally woken up!

We weren't in the greatest situation, but I was still really happy to see Mr. Delgado. It was a big relief to finally talk about what was going on with an adult I liked and trusted. Maybe Mr. Delgado could help us figure out how to get out of here.

I could tell Josh felt the same way, because for the first five minutes Mr. Delgado couldn't get a word into the conversation. Josh and I were too busy telling him about Professor Chronos, Emmitt, and the doubles.

"Where is the professor now?" Mr. Delgado asked.

"He's in there, sleeping with the others," I answered, gesturing at the MemoryFile door. The three of us looked through the door at the rows of motionless computer-animated figures—men and women, boys and girls. We wondered how they had all fallen into the clutches of Emmitt. We'd probably never know, because we were almost never awake at the same time.

"Well, at least that explains what's been happening to me," Mr. Delgado said when we were done. "I'm afraid I made the same mistake you did, Chris. When I came upon the TimeSolvers Web site on the Internet, I took the quiz, too. But I never even got to meet my double. I went to sleep that night, and the next morning when I woke up, I was in here. Emmitt must have made the switch during the night."

"What do you think we should do?" Josh asked.

"Yeah," I jumped in. "Now that you know what's going on, how do you think we should get out of here?"

Mr. Delgado shrugged. He looked tired, as if he could hardly keep his eyes open. "I'm afraid I don't have a clue," he murmured dreamily. "I never was too big on computers, as you know. I'm afraid all this stuff about deleting files doesn't make much sense to me. If Jenna erases Emmitt's memory, it might help, but it might also destroy the only mind that knows how to get us out of here."

"That's what I was thinking, too," Josh seconded sadly.

Mr. Delgado yawned. I noticed that he was starting to look sort of blurry around the edges. Then his head bobbed forward and his eyes closed.

"Mr. Delgado, wake up!" I shouted.

He raised his head and opened his eyes. "Sorry," he said apologetically. "Now what were we talking about? Oh, yes, getting out of here." He took a deep breath. "I wish I had some bright idea, but I don't," he mumbled. "Frankly, when you started telling me the story, I was hoping you kids had a plan." He looked at Josh. "You're into computers, aren't you?"

"Yeah, but programming them is different from being part of one," Josh said. "And this program is so strange. I don't know what'll happen if we erase Emmitt. We might erase ourselves along with him."

Mr. Delgado nodded and closed his eyes again. I suddenly noticed that I could see right through him.

"Mr. Delgado!" I yelled again, but it was no good. He was dissolving right in front of my eyes. I glanced through the door of the MemoryFile and saw that he was back in his box.

I shivered even though I didn't feel cold. That was the one good thing about being an animated cartoon figure, I decided: you didn't get hot or cold or hungry, only tired. Still, I would have given anything to be a real three-dimensional person once more.

"I guess Mr. Delgado's being read again," I said to Josh.

"Yeah." He nodded. "I wonder why he's always getting read but we're not?"

"Probably because it's hard for his double to fake being a music teacher," I guessed. "After all, Mr. Delgado can play fifteen different instruments. It would take a few days for Emmitt to learn all that."

"And the spring concert is coming up tomorrow night," Josh speculated. "Mr. Delgado's double is probably getting ready to conduct the band."

"Yeah . . ." I said wistfully. I was thinking how excited I'd been about performing my trumpet solos. I'd figured everyone would be blown away when they heard my smooth sound. Now I'd never get the chance to show them how well I could play.

Anger flared through me. I marched back and forth across the template. Then I saw a small key off to the side. I leaned over it.

Fax, it read.

"Hey, what does this key do?" I asked.

Josh took a look at it. "Sometimes I can't believe you're so dense about computers, Chris," he growled. "That key allows you to fax stuff through the modem over phone lines. Say you want to send—" He broke off, and a grin slid across his face. "Chris!" he declared. "You know what? You're a genius."

"Huh?" I looked at him, puzzled.

"Don't you get it—?" he began, but before he could tell me what there was to get, we heard the now familiar click of the computer being switched on. I held my breath. Who would be looking at us now? I was hoping it was Jenna, but somehow I knew it wouldn't be. Not after Emmitt had caught her trying to communicate with us.

As the bright light flooded in, I lifted my head. When I saw the face peering at us, I swallowed.

It was Mr. Delgado, the fake one, and he had a look in his eyes that would have made my blood freeze—had I been real.

"Hmm," murmured the fake Mr. Delgado, otherwise known as Emmitt. "Someone left the MemoryFile open, I see. The professor is asleep as usual, and so is the music teacher. But you boys are awake—again. I'll have to correct that."

The fake Mr. Delgado pressed a few buttons on the keyboard. Immediately that all-too-familiar pins-and-needles feeling traveled along my arms and legs.

"Enjoy your sleep, kids," the fake Mr. Delgado hissed. "It'll be the last one you have before you're erased permanently."

I opened my eyes wide. "What does he mean 'erased permanently'?" I yelled to Josh.

Josh didn't answer. Then the fake Mr. Delgado spoke again. "A little more reading of the music teacher," he said, an evil smile curving over his lips, "and I, Emmitt, will have all the information I need to be you—all of you—forever!"

I could feel my eyelids sinking down, but I fought it as hard as I could. I had to. If Emmitt was telling the truth, we had to do something fast.

"Josh," I shouted. "Get up! Don't go to sleep. Whatever you do, don't go to sleep!"

The fake Mr. Delgado frowned. "I don't understand. You should be out cold by now," he murmured. Then he snapped his fingers. "Your doubles—that's it! It's late for a school night, and your doubles must be sleeping! That's making you two much too awake. I'll have to see about that tomorrow, after I finish reading the music teacher." My stomach churned madly as the fake Mr. Delgado laughed. "Don't worry. As soon as I'm finished with him, I'll say good-night to all of you—for good."

The screen went dark.

Almost instantly, the pins-and-needles feeling faded. I turned to Josh, my eyes wide.

"How do we stop him from erasing us permanently?" I asked frantically.

Josh wiggled his hands and didn't say anything for a moment. I could tell he was afraid to let me know the truth. "We can't stop him, Chris," he finally admitted. "Not unless Jenna comes back on-line before it's too late."

We stared at each other.

How much time did we have left?

Chapter 20

I don't know how long we sat there. Probably for most of the night and all of the next morning. We didn't talk much. There didn't seem to be much point. We couldn't try to fax Jenna or anyone else while the computer was turned off. As bad as being stuck in a computer was, the thought of being totally erased was a zillion times worse. I kept thinking about my mom and dad and Eddie, and I wondered if they'd even noticed that the Chris they'd been living with for the past day and a half wasn't me.

They'd always complained about how disorganized and messy I was. Maybe they'd rather have Emmitt around. Emmitt was definitely tidy and well-organized. But then again, he was a total creep, too.

To my surprise, later that day the professor suddenly appeared beside us.

"Boys, you look upset," he said. "Tell me what's wrong. What's been going on?"

We told him as quickly as we could. The professor tugged at his beard. "We can't let him get away with this!" he shouted.

"Who's going to stop him?" I asked. I wanted to be more positive about things, but I couldn't. I had a bad feeling that time was running out, and I was right. A minute later, I heard a click.

The screen filled with light, and a giant face looked in at us.

This time it was my face again—Emmitt disguised as me.

"Hello," he said, grinning nastily. Through the thick glass of the screen, the room beyond was a blur, but I could recognize that it was my room—and it was perfectly clean. Everything was put away, and the surfaces were probably all dusted and polished, too.

Just looking at it made me mad. "Who do you think you are, you monster?" I screamed.

But my double couldn't understand what I was saying any more than Jenna had been able to. He just stared at us gleefully.

Then he focused his attention on me. "Guess who'll be playing the trumpet solos in a few hours at the spring concert," he said in a taunting voice. "Not you." He started to laugh—creepy, high-pitched laughter.

Suddenly I saw a flash of color beside me. I turned my head. The computer-animated Mr. Delgado—the real one—was standing there, blinking. My heart sank. That meant that Emmitt had finished reading my music teacher, and now he was ready to erase us!

As my double leaned over the keyboard, striking keys, I stood there, too terrified to move. Emmitt was about to dissolve me, Josh, Mr. Delgado, and everyone else inside the computer into a million particles. And there wasn't a single thing we could do about it.

But then something came over me. I couldn't just stand there and let him destroy us.

"Nyah, nyah," I said, sticking out my tongue at

Emmitt. I knew I was being childish—he couldn't even hear me—but so what? It felt great. "You think you're human," I taunted, "but you're really just a stupid computer chip."

"Chris," Josh warned.

"You don't even know how to be human, you dumb machine!" I jeered.

Emmitt's face darkened with rage. Maybe he couldn't hear me, but he could figure out he was being mocked just by looking at my face and gestures. Then he smiled again. "Go ahead and play your games," he said smugly. "In a minute, my friend, you'll be history." He pressed a button on the keyboard.

I heard a loud click. *This is the end,* I thought. But I was still there. I stared up at the screen. Then my mouth dropped open.

The screen had split in two. Half of it was filled with my face—well, Emmitt's face—and the other half was filled with Jenna's.

"Jenna!" Josh and I shouted at the same time.

Jenna looked scared. "Josh, or whoever he is, is in the shower getting ready for the concert," she whispered. "So I don't have much time, okay?"

I glanced nervously at the face of my double on the other half of the screen. What would Emmitt do now that Jenna had shown up?

"It's cool, Chris," Josh said. "She's on a different computer. Even Emmitt can't see through walls. Look at him. He has no idea she's there."

I examined the face of my double. It was true. Emmitt looked perfectly calm and smug. Then I noticed he was still typing commands into the computer—fast!

"What's he doing?" Mr. Delgado demanded.

"He's erasing us," the professor replied sadly.

"Let him," Josh said. "I have a plan." He turned to Jenna.

Jenna had clicked on *List Subfiles*. Now she brought the cursor to the subfile *Ttimme*.

"Do you guys still want me to erase this?" she asked, gesturing at the file.

I nodded *yes* as hard as I could. Jenna looked uncertain. I looked over at Josh. He was shaking his head vigorously—*no!*

"Josh, what's wrong with you?" I yelled. "Erasing Emmitt is our only chance! We've got to erase him before he erases us!"

Then I saw what Josh was doing. He was flashing at Jenna the command *Delete main file*. At the same time he clicked on a modem command so that the words *Transmit file* were also flashing up on the screen.

"I don't get it," Jenna said. "Do you want me to erase the whole file or fax it?"

"Both," Josh mouthed at her.

For a moment, I didn't think Jenna understood, but then she nodded and said, "Where to?"

"Jump on the *Home* key, Chris," Josh commanded me.

I jumped. The words *Go home* filled the screen.

Jenna hesitated. "You want me to fax the file to our house?" she asked doubtfully.

Josh nodded again. "Yes," he mouthed. "And hurry!"

Still Jenna hesitated. She looked as if she wasn't sure what buttons to hit first. On the other side of the split screen, the question *Erase all files? Yes/No* had appeared. Emmitt was reading it, his fingers poised over the keyboard.

I forgot all about feeling brave. A bolt of terror passed through me, and I started screaming.

Emmitt had almost finished what he was doing.

We were about to be erased!

Josh waved at Jenna. "Now!" he shrieked. "Do it now!"

Chapter 21

Everything got very confusing then. I saw the screen split a third time. For a brief second I caught a glimpse of Mr. Broadus's face. He was scowling, as usual. "What's this silly game doing on my computer?" I heard him bellow.

Then I couldn't hear anything from outside the computer anymore, because inside tons of different voices were crowding through the air like radio waves. Around me the sleeping figures from the MemoryFile were waking up and flying through the air like ghosts. I felt them sweep past me like rushing wind. Then they were gone.

I saw millions of tiny particles of light floating through total blackness. I felt as if I were sliding through the Milky Way, or lost in an unknown galaxy somewhere in outer space. I could still hear voices, but they sounded more distant now. Then I looked down and saw that I had vanished. I could still see a faint outline of a boy, a figure traced in glimmering particles of light, but as I watched, even that disappeared. I had no arms, no legs.

Oh, no! Panic rushed through me. *So this is what it's like to be erased,* I thought. I tried to shout, but I couldn't. I didn't have a head or a mouth anymore. Still, I heard a far-off voice that sounded like mine. "Josh, Jenna, Mr. Delgado, Professor Chronos, Mom, Dad, Eddie . . . bye-bye!" I felt as if I were moving faster and faster toward some unknown black hole. Then I felt something else. Pain.

It stunned me. Ever since I'd been a live-action cartoon in the computer, nothing had hurt me. When I'd banged into the page break or pinched myself trying to stay awake, I hadn't felt it at all. But now I hurt all over.

I looked down and grinned. I had legs. I had arms. And I had a head. I knew this because I'd just banged it into something very hard!

"Ouch!" I yelped.

I rubbed my forehead. I had smacked my head on the corner of a table. My computer table at home! I blinked. I was standing in the fading twilight in my own—now very clean—room.

Josh's plan had worked!

I looked around and realized I was alone. But that made sense, didn't it? After all, if all of the people in the MemoryFile were faxed through the air, and Emmitt's TimeSolvers Web site was erased, where would we go but back into our own bodies? That meant that Josh was back in his room with Jenna, Mr. Delgado was probably at school getting ready for the concert, and Professor Chronos was in the lab at the university. At least, that's what I hoped.

I pinched myself hard.

It definitely hurt. I grinned again. I was real.

Then a horrible though occurred to me. When we were faxed out of the computer, Emmitt's memory file had been faxed with us. That meant Emmitt must have gone somewhere—but where? I shuddered and glanced anxiously at my computer screen.

File erased, it read.

I breathed a sigh of relief. *Emmitt's gone!* I told myself. I was about to click *Exit* and log off the Internet when a message window appeared on my screen. I clicked on the window and a ribbon of letters danced across the monitor.

Chris, are you there?

I'm here. Who's this? I typed back.

It's Josh and Jenna.

Where are you guys? I asked.

We're at home, like you, one of them answered.

Is everything okay?

It looks like it, they replied. *I guess we won't know for sure until we get to school and find out if Mr. Delgado got back all right.*

I hope the professor's okay, too, I typed in. *And everyone else Emmitt took over.* I hesitated a moment, then added, *Josh, how did you know faxing the file would work?*

Josh didn't answer right away. *I didn't,* he typed back at last. *But I figured Emmitt had to have modified one of the existing functions on the computer to get us in there in the first place. I decided he must have modified the scan function and used it to copy us onto the machine. But that still meant he must have used some version of a fax transmission, otherwise there couldn't have been any molecular transubstantiation.*

Any what? I interrupted. As usual, Josh had lost me with his technical-speak.

Molecules, electrons moving through the air. See, somehow Emmitt modified the program so it could actually break people down into molecules and reassemble them in cartoon form in cyberspace. Get it?

Yeah, I typed back. *I get it.* I didn't, but I wasn't about to tell Josh that.

So I took a gamble that he'd fiddled with the modem, Josh continued. *If you wanted to put someone on a computer or take them off, that would be the most likely way to do it. I still don't really have any idea how Emmitt rigged it, though. I guess I probably never will. In a way, it's too bad we got rid of him—*

No, it isn't, I answered. I suddenly remembered what I'd been thinking about just before Josh and Jenna e-mailed me. The message on my screen had said *File erased,* but . . .

How do we know Emmitt is really gone? I typed. *Could he have been sent over the fax, too?*

Yeah, but he had nowhere to go, Josh replied. *Remember what the professor said? He had turned himself into a computer program. The only way for Emmitt to have a physical presence in the world was to take over people— like us. When Jenna transmitted our minds and memories back through the modem, we took over our own bodies again. Emmitt didn't have a body to return to. I guess maybe he could be floating around in the air someplace, but I doubt it.*

I hope you're right, I typed.

Me, too, Josh replied. *But then again, I'd love to know how he did all that stuff. I mean, the programming was incredible. The professor said even he didn't have a clue how Emmitt managed to write a program that could do all that stuff. The guy was definitely a genius.*

He was also a creep, I reminded Josh. *Besides, I bet you'll figure it out. After all, you're a genius, too.*

You think so?

Jenna started typing before I could reply. *He's going to be a late genius if you two don't stop talking,* she reminded us. *The concert starts in two hours.*

That's right, I typed back.

Are you ready to play some awesome trumpet, Chris? Josh asked.

You bet, I answered. *Later, dudes.*

I'm not a dude, Jenna flamed me back.

I laughed as I reached up to switch off my computer. Just then, my mom poked her head into my room. "Chris, you'd better start getting ready. You're supposed to be at school to rehearse pretty soon."

I flashed her a big smile. "Don't worry, Mom. I'm totally on top of my schedule."

"I've heard that before," Mom murmured, closing the door.

I pulled off my T-shirt and jeans and put on a white shirt and dark pants. I was starting to feel nervous. Normally, I would have spent every free minute practicing like a lunatic, but I'd been too busy being stuck in Emmitt's warped computer program. I wondered if my double had practiced.

Probably not. Emmitt didn't seem like the musical type. What if I totally blew my solos?

Then I smiled. I repeated aloud something Mr. Delgado often said: "A musician who doesn't practice just has to get inspired."

That was it—I was going to be inspired.

I ran out of my room and bounded down the stairs. "Inspired," I repeated to myself. I was concentrating so hard on being inspired, I almost tripped over Eddie, who was sitting on the bottom step reading one of his dumb dinosaur books.

"Hey, don't sit on the bottom of the stairs, okay, dorkface?" I said, and I rumpled his hair.

He looked at me and stuck out his tongue. "Okay, double-dorkface," he shot back. Then he smiled. I had the feeling Eddie was almost happy I'd insulted him.

I raced into the kitchen. Dinner was over, and Dad was reading the paper while Mom sipped a cup of coffee. Dad looked up as I came in. "Oh, Chris," he said. Then he cleared his throat. "I know you're on your way to the rehearsal, but Mom and I wanted to talk to you about something."

"Yeah?" I said, my heart skipping a beat. Had my "perfect" double somehow managed to get me in trouble?

"We think it's great that you've finally taken to heart all the things we've been saying about being neat and well-organized . . ." Dad went on.

"I was just thrilled that you cleaned your room this afternoon," Mom chimed in.

"But . . .?" I said.

"But, Chris." My dad put down his paper. "You shouldn't forget to be yourself."

"To be honest, you've been pretty obnoxious today," Mom added softly.

"Obnoxious?" I said. I felt like laughing out loud!

"Yes, kind of bossy and know-it-all," Mom continued. "I didn't appreciate it when you said that I was incredibly inefficient when I was making dinner tonight."

"I said that?"

My dad nodded sternly.

"Yeah, and after school you told me my intelligence was mediocre," Eddie said as he strolled into the kitchen. "I don't know what that means, but I know it's not nice."

"The point is that you haven't seemed like yourself for the last two days," my dad went on.

"What did I seem like?" I couldn't resist asking.

"Weird and nasty," Eddie replied immediately. "On top of being dorky," he added.

"Well, I don't think your intelligence is mediocre," I told him. I looked at Mom. "And no way are you incredibly inefficient. Look, I'm really sorry for whatever I said, all right? I've had a lot on my mind, and I guess I wasn't really myself."

Mom smiled. "I know you're nervous about the concert, but I'm glad you're back to normal, Chris."

"Me, too," I said.

"I hope we haven't upset you," she added. "We just wanted to clear the air."

"You didn't upset me one bit," I answered honestly. I'd really been worried that my family might rather have Emmitt around than me. And now I knew that wasn't true. They thought he was an obnoxious creep, just like I did.

I smiled. Emmitt may have stolen my body, but he'd never been able to take my spirit. And as crazy and awful as the last two days had been, I'd learned something important. I really liked myself, and that was what mattered most. Suddenly, I had all the inspiration I needed.

"Why don't you head over to school now, Chris?" Mom suggested, planting a kiss on my forehead. "We'll drive over in a little while for the big event."

"Okay. Wish me luck!" I called as I sprinted toward the front door. I swung it open wide and raced down the street toward school, but halfway down the block, I had to turn around and go back.

"Mom!" I screamed as I pounded on the front door. "Mom! Open up!"

She hurriedly unlocked the door and peered out. "Chris, what is it?"

"I forgot my trumpet!"

Chapter 22

When I ran into the school building, I found Jenna and Josh standing outside the auditorium with a familiar-looking person.

"Mr. Delgado!" I gasped happily.

"Chris!" Mr. Delgado winked at me. "Good to have you back." Then he became serious. "Did you get any time to practice your solos?"

I became serious, too. "Sorry, Mr. Delgado."

"Of course you didn't." Mr. Delgado shook his head sympathetically. Then he winked at me again. "Well, remember what I always say—"

"'A musician who doesn't practice just has to get inspired!'" Josh and I chorused.

"And after what happened to us, I'm definitely inspired," I added. "I'm psyched to have my own life back."

"Me, too," Josh put in.

Mr. Delgado smiled. "That makes three of us. Let's go into the auditorium."

Inside, the rest of the band was already in place for rehearsal.

Mr. Delgado clapped his hands, and everyone fell silent. "All right, everyone, get out your instruments. The concert begins in forty-five minutes, so we'll have time for a quick run-through. Ms. March, can you give us a C?"

My history teacher, who always played piano for our band concerts, nodded and hit C.

We all got busy tuning our instruments—at least, those of us who had instruments that needed tuning. All I did was tighten my mouthpiece and polish my trumpet with my shirt sleeve. Then Mr. Delgado lifted his baton, and we went into the first piece.

A short while later, after we had played several of the songs through, the auditorium filled up with families and teachers who'd come to see the concert. At a little before eight, I saw my family come in and find seats way in the back. As soon as my mom spotted me onstage, she jumped up and started frantically waving her arms to get my attention. A few days before, I would have been majorly embarrassed and pretended I didn't see her. But tonight I felt so good that I stood up and waved back to her in full view of all of my friends.

So what if everyone thinks I'm a nerd? I thought. *At least I'm a real, live, three-dimensional nerd!*

"Okay, everyone," Mr. Delgado said softly. "It's just about time." A second later, the lights of the auditorium went down, and our principal, Ms. Baker, stepped up to the podium. "Welcome, everyone, to the Jackson Middle School spring concert. Before we begin, our band teacher, Mr. Delgado, would like to say a few words."

Mr. Delgado bounded up to the microphone. "I'd like to say that we're all happy to have you here, and we hope you'll enjoy our music. Tonight Chris Fenton will be playing two solos on trumpet, and—" he grinned as he turned around to look at me for a second—"something tells me it will be a truly inspired performance," he finished.

Sure enough, when it came time to play my solos, I didn't miss a note. The applause was deafening, and I felt great.

"Way to go, Chris," Josh whispered.

Take that, Emmitt, I thought. *I'd like to see you play a trumpet with that much feeling!*

I was still beaming when the concert ended and everyone came up to congratulate us. I stood up to greet my family, who were making their way to the stage.

Just then I felt a hand on my shoulder.

I whirled around. There was Mr. Broadus.

Chapter 23

"Hello, Chris," Mr. Broadus said. "I just wanted to congratulate you on your performance." His eyes flashed. "You kept time very well," he added.

"Uh, thanks, Mr. Broadus," I replied.

"Time must never be wasted, don't you agree?" Mr. Broadus continued softly. He tightened his grip on my shoulder.

"Owww," I said. I looked up at him. Mr. Broadus was smiling, but he didn't look friendly.

"Why don't you come with me to my office now?" he said. "I'm sure we have a lot to talk about."

"Like what?" I demanded. I tried to wriggle out of his grasp, but I couldn't.

I looked around frantically. Josh was talking to his mom and dad, and Jenna was talking to my mom and dad.

I looked back up at Mr. Broadus. His eyes were gleaming strangely, and there was a hard, cold look in them that I recognized! "Emmitt!" I breathed. Suddenly I remembered what I'd seen as I was being transmitted out of the computer: Mr. Broadus staring at his computer screen in bewilderment. Now I knew where Emmitt had gone.

"Where's Mr. Broadus?" I hissed. "What have you done with him?"

"Mr. Broadus is right here with me, but he's used to obeying orders." Emmitt grinned.

I tried to break away again, but it was no good.

"Josh, Josh!" I shouted. "Look who's here! It's our friend Emmitt!"

Josh's head snapped up. His eyes widened. "Mr. Broadus?" he mouthed.

Mr. Broadus—or rather, Emmitt—didn't let me answer. He pulled me toward the side exit of the auditorium. "Just a nice friendly chat, you and I," he said.

I closed my eyes. Josh understood. I hoped he would think of something fast.

But I had a feeling our double troubles were just beginning!

Don't miss any of these exciting books!